ETERNAL ECHOES

A Timeless Journey of Love, Loss, and Hope across the Ages

MUJAHID BAKHT

1

EBook ISBN: 979-8-89302-059-5

Paperback ISBN: 979-8-89302-057-1

Hardcover ISBN: 979-8-89302-058-8

Published By:

ATLAS AMAZON, LLC.

244 Fifth Avenue, D210, New York, N.Y.

United States of America

SECOND EDITION

TABLE OF CONTENTS

4

ABOUT THE AUTHOR

LIFE HISTORY: Mr. Bakhtis a mature, experienced, excessively enthusiastic, energetic administrator with thirty-eight years of proven experience as a businessman in international marketing and public relations. Mr. Bakht is an International Real Estate Specialist and Professional Business and Projects Consultant and Advisor. He was born in Pakistan and educated in Pakistan and the USA. Presently, American Citizen belongs to a business-oriented family. Thirty-eight years Resident of New York, USA.

BUSINESS HISTORY: Mr. Bakht is a Founder and President of Atlas Amazon, LLC., Mr. Bakht is a business developer and multilingual business specialist in the Caribbean, South East Asia, and the Middle East emerging markets Mr. Bakht has served, met, and hosted many heads of the States. Also, maintain a close relationship with investors of high net worth in the USA.

CAREER: Mr. Bakht has been engaged with many multinational companies in the fields of international real estate investment, communication, technology, diamond, gold, mining, Pre-Feb housing, wind and solar energy, outsourcing management, and project consulting, along with business partners and associates worldwide. Mr. Bakht has participated in major national and international conferences, including participated in United Nations (U.N.O.) conferences.

TRAVEL: Mr. Bakht is well-traveled and has visited many countries around the world.

MANAGEMENT EXPERIENCE: Thirty-eight years of diversified experience in project consulting, marketing, and business management. As a Director of Marketing, Director of Public Relations, Director of International Affairs, Executive Vice President, President, CEO, and Chairman of many national and multinational companies. Mr. Bakht hired and trained many professionals as business consultants in international marketing and supervised them.

CERTIFICATE OF ACHIEVEMENT: The Achievement Award was presented to Mr. Bakht by Stephen Fossler for five years of continued growth and customer satisfaction from 1996 to 2001.

HONORS MEMBER:Madison Who's Who of Professionals, having demonstrated exemplary achievement and distinguished contributions to the business community, registered at the Library of Congress in Washington D.C. USA. (2007 and 2008)

HONORS MEMBER: Premiere Who's Who International, professional business executive having demonstrated exemplary achievement and distinguished contributions to the International business community, 2008 and 2009.

CERTIFICATES: Certificate of Authenticity from Bill Rodham Clinton, President of the United States, and Hillary Rodham Clinton First Lady, USA. (July 20, 2000);

CERTIFICATE OF AUTHENTICITY: from Terence R. McAuliffe, Chairman of Democratic National Committee, Tom Dachle, Senate Democratic Leader, Dick Gephardt, House Democratic Leader, USA. (June 16, 2001);

CERTIFICATE OF AUTHENTICITY: from Terence R. McAuliffe, Chairman of Democratic National Committee, USA. (April 16, 2002).

CHAPTER 1

The Enigmatic Bookstore Owner

Rachel Sullivan unlocked the front door of her little shop, "Past Pages," before the city was fully awake. The air outside still felt cool, but inside, the bookstore was warm and filled with the soft, sweet scent of old paper and polished wood. Shelves stood tall on every wall, packed with books so old their covers had faded and their pages had turned the color of tea.

Rachel loved this quiet moment before anyone else arrived. She ran her hand along a row of books and felt the gentle bumps of embossed letters beneath her fingers. Every book in her store had a story—not just inside its pages, but in the way it looked, smelled, and even how it ended up here. She often wondered how many secrets waited on these shelves, just waiting for the right person to pick them up.

Rachel herself was a mystery to most people in the neighborhood. She had bright red hair that curled around her face and clear, curious eyes. She dressed simply, but there was always something thoughtful and careful about the way she moved, as if every small thing mattered. She didn't talk much about her past, but she worked hard every day, dusting the shelves, making tea for her customers, and helping people find the stories they needed—even if they didn't know it yet.

"Past Pages" was more than just a shop; it was a safe place for anyone who needed to get away from the noise of the world. Some people came in to find rare books. Others simply liked to sit in the old green chair in the corner and read. There was even a stray cat that sometimes wandered in and curled up by the radiator. Rachel never chased him away.

But what made "Past Pages" truly special was something nobody could see—not at first. There was an air of mystery here, as if time moved differently inside these walls. Sometimes, Rachel would find things hidden in the books: old letters, pressed flowers, even a photograph or two. She kept these little treasures in a wooden box behind the counter, wondering about the people who left them behind.

8

She often told herself that one day, something extraordinary might happen in her shop. She didn't know how right she was. As she flipped the sign on the door to "Open," Rachel had no idea that her quiet world was about to change forever—and that the biggest secret of her life was waiting just around the corner, between the shelves of "Past Pages."

Rachel loved rare books more than anything else in the world. Whenever she held an old book in her hands, she felt like she was holding a secret from the past. The crackle of the pages, the smell of old paper, and the faded words always made her heart feel light. Each rare book in her shop was like a lost treasure, waiting for the right person to find it.

Most days, Rachel preferred to be alone. She liked the soft quiet in her shop, the gentle sound of pages turning, and the safe feeling of being surrounded by stories. She would lose herself for hours reading a letter she found in a book or studying an old map tucked between the pages. While other people enjoyed parties or busy streets, Rachel was happiest sitting in a corner, a book in her lap, her mind wandering far away.

Her dreams often drifted beyond the walls of "Past Pages." Sometimes, she imagined living in another time or discovering a book that would change her life. She believed there was magic in words—magic that could carry her away from the world outside, at least for a little while.

Though Rachel often felt like an outsider, she didn't mind. Her life was quiet and straightforward, but it was full of wonder. Deep inside, she hoped that someday, something unexpected would happen—something only a true dreamer would notice.

And, in the silence of her little shop, with moonlight shining through the windows and rare books all around, it seemed just possible that the next great story was already waiting for her, somewhere among the shadows and dust.

Rachel's love for stories was more than just a hobby. Stories were her shelter. They were the only thing that had never left her. Long before she opened "Past Pages," Rachel learned that people and places could disappear in an instant, but the worlds inside books always waited for her return.

As a little girl, Rachel lived with her mother in a small, sunlit apartment above a bakery. She remembered the way her mother's laughter filled the rooms, the smell of fresh bread drifting upstairs, and the safety she felt falling asleep while her mother read fairy tales at her bedside. But that happy time didn't last. One cold winter night, her mother became very sick, and after weeks in the hospital, she was gone. Rachel was only ten years old.

The loss was so sudden, Rachel could hardly understand it. She went to live with her aunt, a woman who cared for her but never really understood her. The new house was quiet—too quiet. Rachel found it hard to talk about her mother, and it was easier just to stay silent. When the world felt empty, she would escape into books, hiding in the stories as if they were secret doorways to better places.

Rachel's father was never in the picture. She never knew where he went or why he left. Her mother only told her once, "Sometimes people leave, but stories stay. You can always open a book and find your way home." After her mother died, those words became Rachel's shield. Even when she felt invisible at school or lost at family gatherings, she knew she could always return to the pages of her favorite stories.

Through the years, Rachel moved from one place to another. She had to say goodbye to old friends and start over again and again. Each time she packed her small suitcase, the first thing she wrapped in soft cloth was her little box of books. Fairy tales, mysteries, poems—each one held a piece of the home she missed. She would read the same books over and over, finding comfort in the familiar words and the feeling that she belonged somewhere, even if only in her imagination.

When Rachel grew up, she dreamed of having a place that would never change—a place filled with stories and memories that nobody could take from her. That's why she opened "Past Pages." The bookstore was more than a business; it was her way of building a home that couldn't be lost. Each book on the shelves reminded her that every ending could also be a beginning.

Even as an adult, Rachel still felt the ache of her early losses, but she never let it turn her cold. Instead, she shared her love of books with everyone who walked into her shop. She listened to their stories, too, and sometimes helped them find a story that matched their heartbreak or hope. Deep down, she believed that books could heal, and that somewhere between the lines, there was always a new chance to start again.

Rachel's past was full of things she wished she could change, but when she looked at her bookstore, she saw proof that loss could lead to something beautiful. Still, in her heart, she wondered if life might one day give her a story all her own—something precious and lasting, like the stories she treasured most.

It was a rainy Tuesday morning when Rachel noticed the small brown box by the bookstore's door. She almost missed it, tucked between the umbrella stand and the old welcome mat. There was no return address, only her name written in careful, dark letters: "Rachel Sullivan, Past Pages."

Rachel paused, frowning a little. She hadn't ordered any books lately. Most deliveries came with big stickers or company logos, not quiet boxes like this one. For a moment, she just stared at it, feeling a strange flutter in her chest. The shop was still empty, just the low hum of the heater and the gentle tap of rain against the window.

She picked up the box. It was heavier than it looked. The tape was neat, the paper plain. She set it on the counter and slowly peeled back the tape, careful not to tear anything. Her hands shook a little. She told herself it was just curiosity, but deep inside, something felt different about this package—like a secret waiting to be discovered.

Inside, wrapped in thin brown paper, were two old books and a bundle of yellowed envelopes tied with blue string. The books looked ancient, their covers cracked and edges soft. Rachel ran her fingers across them, feeling the rough leather and gold letters. She opened the top book and found a pressed flower between its pages—a faded rose, as delicate as a sigh.

But it was the bundle of letters that made her heart pound. They looked fragile, the paper almost see-through with age. The top envelope had her name on it—"Rachel." She blinked, surprised. Who would send her letters this old? She didn't recognize the handwriting. It was beautiful and strange, the kind of penmanship people used long ago.

Rachel turned one envelope over in her hand, holding it to the light. There was no stamp, no address, only the name "James Thornton" written on the back. The name didn't mean anything to her, but it sent a chill up her spine. The more she looked at the letters, the more she felt as if she was being watched—or as if someone from the past was trying to speak to her.

She glanced toward the door, almost expecting to see someone standing there. But the street outside was empty except for the rain. Rachel carefully untied the blue string, trying not to tear the old paper. She opened the first letter and unfolded the page. The handwriting danced across the sheet, neat and slanted.

As she read, a strange feeling settled over her—part hope, part fear. The letter spoke of longing, of dreams, and of someone searching for her through the years. It was signed, simply, "Yours always, James Thornton."

Rachel didn't know what to think. She felt caught between two worlds—the safe, quiet bookstore and a mystery much older than herself. She glanced again at the unopened letters and the rain outside. Something had changed. She could feel it in her bones.

This was no ordinary delivery. It was the start of a story she had never expected to find.

Rachel sat at her desk, the bundle of old letters in her lap. The bookstore was quiet except for the ticking of the clock and the distant sound of rain. She turned over the first envelope again, her eyes caught by the graceful way her name was written—"Rachel." Something was haunting about it, as if the writer had known her for a very long time.

With a deep breath, she opened the letter. The paper was thin and crisp, the ink faded but still easy to read. The handwriting was beautiful, old-fashioned, and each word was carefully formed. Rachel felt her heart beat faster as she read the opening line:

"My dearest Rachel,

11

If you are reading this, then the impossible has happened. Our words have finally crossed the borders of time…"

She stopped, rereading the sentence. The borders of time? Rachel shook her head, wondering if it was some kind of story or a trick. But the letter didn't sound like a joke. There was something about the words that felt real and urgent, as if the writer was truly reaching out to her.

The letter continued:

"I have searched for you through the years and shadows. I have left these letters hoping they would find you, wherever you may be. Do you remember the blue lamp in your window, or the garden where you once read in the sun? Sometimes, when the world is quiet, I hear your laughter, and it reminds me why I must keep trying."

Rachel's breath caught. She did have a blue lamp in her bedroom window, a gift from her mother when she was small. And the garden—she used to hide there with her books on sunny days, long ago. How could a stranger know these details? She felt a prickling at the back of her neck, a tingle of fear and wonder.

The letter was signed, "Yours always, James Thornton." Rachel let the paper fall to the desk. Her hands were shaking. Was this some elaborate trick, or had someone been watching her? She felt exposed, like a secret part of her heart had been put on display.

She opened another envelope. This one was dated from the past—almost fifty years ago. Again, it began, "My beloved Rachel," and the words seemed to flow straight into her mind. Each letter held clues only she would understand—childhood memories, old dreams, even her favorite book as a girl.

The air in the bookstore felt suddenly heavy, charged with something she couldn't name. As she turned the pages, a cold draft swept through the room, fluttering the letters and making the shadows dance. Rachel looked around, feeling as if someone invisible stood beside her, waiting for her to read the following line.

Was it possible? Was someone reaching out to her from another time? The thought sent chills through her, but she couldn't stop reading. The letters seemed to know her deepest thoughts, her fears, and even her hopes.

With every word, the world Rachel knew began to shift, and the first threads of something supernatural started to wrap around her quiet life, changing everything forever.

CHAPTER 2

The Discovery

— ∞ —

Rachel sat behind the counter, the mysterious package open in front of her. She gently pushed aside the old books and turned her attention to the bundle of letters. The paper felt thin and delicate, so old that it seemed almost ready to fall apart. Rachel's hands trembled as she untied the blue string that held the letters together.

She laid the letters out on the desk, lining them up by date. Some envelopes were yellowed and stained at the corners, others looked almost new. Rachel noticed the handwriting was always the same—beautiful, slanted, and neat. Each one was addressed to her, even the letters written decades ago.

As she worked, Rachel searched the rest of the box for clues. She found a tiny pressed flower inside one book—a rose, perfectly dried. There was also an old photograph, black and white, showing a man in a suit standing beside a large clock. On the back, someone had written, "For Rachel, always in time. – J.T."

Rachel's curiosity grew. Who was J.T.? Could it be James Thornton, the man who signed the letters? Her mind raced with questions. How could anyone know so much about her life? Was it possible these were meant for someone else, someone with the same name? But as she read a few lines here and there, Rachel realized the letters spoke about her, describing memories and places only she would know.

She opened another book from the package and shook it gently. A folded map slipped out, marked with small red X's and a date circled in blue ink. Rachel tried to remember if she had ever seen this map before. It looked like a part of New York, but some of the street names were different, old-fashioned.

Rachel looked for more details. At the bottom of the box, she found a tiny key taped to a scrap of paper. On the paper, someone had written, "For the green desk drawer." Rachel's heart jumped. Her desk, the one she used every day, had a small green drawer she could never open. She had found it locked the day she bought the shop, and over time, she had forgotten about it.

13

She took the key and hurried to the desk. Her hands shook as she slid it into the tiny lock. It turned smoothly, and with a soft click, the drawer popped open. Inside, she found another letter—older and thinner than the rest. It was addressed to her, just like all the others.

For a moment, Rachel sat very still. She could feel something big was happening, as if a story she had always loved was finally coming to life. The quiet bookshop felt full of hidden eyes and soft whispers. Was this fate, a trick, or something else?

Rachel took a deep breath. She knew she couldn't ignore this mystery. With every letter and every clue, she felt pulled further into the unknown—a world where the past and present might finally meet, and where her own story was just beginning.

Rachel spent the rest of the afternoon reading the letters one by one. As she unfolded each fragile page, she noticed something odd: every letter seemed to mention things that hadn't happened yet—at least, not when the letters were written. The words made her feel as if the writer knew secrets about the world before anyone else.

In one letter dated "April 12, 1974," James Thornton wrote,

"By the time you find this, the city will be alive with music, and the old opera house on Fifth Avenue will shine with new lights."

Rachel looked up, her heart pounding. The opera house had only been restored last year. Before that, it was closed for decades, its lights dark and the doors locked. How could someone in 1974 know about that?

In another letter from 1993, James described a small bakery on the corner of Maple and East, famous for its honey cakes. Rachel smiled, thinking of the bakery near her shop. It had only opened three years ago, but the letter described the owner and even mentioned a golden bell hanging over the door. Rachel had never told anyone about that bell, not even her friends.

The more she read, the more uneasy she felt. Some letters even described moments from her own life. One said,

"I hope you keep the blue lamp by your window. Its gentle glow reminds me that hope is never lost, even on the darkest nights."

Rachel stared at the lamp on her bedside table—the same one she'd had since childhood. No one outside her family even knew it existed. The writer described it in such detail that she felt a cold shiver run down her arms.

Other letters talked about events that hadn't happened yet, at least not to her knowledge. One mentioned a heavy snowfall coming soon and how it would trap her in the shop for a whole day. Another described a book festival that would fill her street with laughter and music, even though the city hadn't announced any plans for a festival.

14

Rachel grew more and more confused. Was this a game? Some clever trick played by a stranger? But the letters felt too personal, too full of tiny truths, to be a simple prank. Every word made her feel as if James Thornton could see through time itself, watching her life as if it were a story he already knew.

She checked the dates and looked for clues, but nothing made sense. The handwriting never changed, and every letter ended the same way:

"Until we meet, remember the rose. Yours always, James."

Rachel placed her hand on the pressed flower she had found in the book earlier. It was a rose, just like the one James mentioned in his letters.

For the first time, Rachel felt both excited and afraid. Someone—or something—was trying to reach her, weaving her life and the future into words written long ago. The question was, how much of her story had already been written, and what secret was she being asked to uncover next?

Rachel could not get the name "James Thornton" out of her mind. She repeated it softly, hoping it would trigger a memory, but it sounded like no one she had ever met. The letters made it feel urgent, as if James was a real person watching over her from the shadows of time. She decided she had to find out the truth.

That night, after she locked up "Past Pages," Rachel sat down at her old laptop. The shop was quiet except for the soft hum of rain against the windows. She typed "James Thornton" into the search bar and hit enter. At first, hundreds of results popped up—authors, scientists, actors, even a mayor from a small town. But none of them seemed right. Most lived far away or were much younger or older than James in their letters.

Rachel tried again, this time adding "New York" and "letters" to her search. A few local news stories appeared, but they were about someone else. She clicked through page after page, but nothing was connecting James Thornton to old letters or mysterious packages.

Not giving up, Rachel dug deeper. She visited online forums about antique books and time capsules. She asked quiet questions under a false name, hoping someone else had found letters like hers. There were plenty of stories—hidden love notes, lost diaries, even messages in bottles—but nobody mentioned James Thornton.

Next, Rachel checked the city archives website. She searched old newspapers, public records, and even obituaries, hoping to spot the familiar handwriting or the name of her mysterious pen pal. She found a few people with the same name, but their lives did not match the clues in the letters. There were no stories of a man leaving strange messages for a woman across decades.

Her last hope was the library. Rachel went early the next morning, carrying the first letter in her coat pocket. She asked the librarian, Mrs. Greene, if she had ever heard of James Thornton. Mrs. Greene shook her head and smiled kindly. "It's a nice name, dear, but I don't remember it."

Rachel showed her the handwriting, asking if she recognized the style. Mrs. Greene looked closely. "It's very old-fashioned, I'll give you that. But there's something special about it. It's almost…timeless."

Rachel felt a chill. Timeless. That was exactly how the letters felt.

She made copies of the oldest letters and left a note on the library's history board, asking if anyone had heard of a James Thornton who wrote to a woman named Rachel. Then she checked the rare books section, searching for clues in old author lists, indexes, and even faded dedication pages.

Everywhere she looked, Rachel found nothing but dead ends and more questions. Yet, every failure only made her more curious. If James Thornton really existed, he was hiding well. If he were a ghost or a trick, he was clever enough to stay invisible.

As Rachel walked back to her shop that evening, her thoughts spun with hope and worry. The truth about James Thornton was out there—she could feel it. She promised herself she would not give up until she found out who, or what, he really was.

After Rachel started looking for James Thornton, small, strange things began to happen around her. At first, she thought she was just tired from all her searching and reading. But soon, even the regular days at "Past Pages" felt different—like the air in the bookstore was charged with a secret she couldn't see.

One morning, Rachel came in to open the shop and found a single white rose on the doormat. There was no note, no sign of who had left it. The rose looked precisely like the pressed flower she had found in the old book. She held it in her hand for a long time, her heart pounding. Maybe it was a simple gift from a customer, she thought. But deep down, she knew it was more than that.

Later that week, she was sorting through a box of secondhand books when she found a novel she had loved as a child—a rare edition that was almost impossible to find. She opened it and gasped. Inside was a bookmark with her name written in handwriting that matched the letters from James. How could it be? She was sure she had never seen that copy before.

Another day, Rachel was walking home from the bakery when she overheard two people talking about the same opera house James had mentioned in his letter—the one with the new lights. They said it was opening for a special midnight concert, something that had never happened before. The hairs on Rachel's arms stood up. Was this just luck? Or was James somehow sending her messages through the world around her?

16

The strangest moment came when Rachel was locking up for the night. As she reached for the light switch, she heard the soft chime of the green desk drawer in her office—the one she had only just opened with the mysterious key. She hurried over, but no one was there. Inside the drawer, she found another note in the same careful handwriting:

"Look for me where the clocks stand still."

Rachel's mind raced. Was someone breaking in to leave her clues? Or was something else guiding her, something not of this world? She checked the security cameras, but they showed nothing out of the ordinary. Still, she could not shake the feeling that she was not alone.

Every day brought a new coincidence. Strangers said her name and then looked confused, as if they had not meant to speak. Old songs from her childhood played on the radio at just the right moment. A letter addressed to "Rachel Sullivan" appeared in her mailbox—no stamp, no sender, just her name and a date circled in red ink. The date was next week.

Rachel began to feel as if she was moving through a story written just for her, with James Thornton as the invisible author. She wanted to be brave, but sometimes the fear made her hands shake. Were these signs warnings or invitations? Was she getting closer to the truth, or being drawn into something she could not control?

Whatever was happening, Rachel knew her quiet life would never be the same. The coincidences were too many, too strange. Someone, or something, was trying to lead her somewhere—and she was no longer sure if she wanted to follow.

Rachel sat in the back room of "Past Pages," the bundle of old letters spread out before her. All around, the shop was silent, but her mind was racing. White roses, secret notes, and strange messages filled her days now. Every part of her wanted to believe it was just chance, but she couldn't shake the feeling that something bigger was happening. The mystery was pulling her in, stronger than any story she had ever read.

For days, Rachel tried to act as if nothing had changed. She smiled at customers, dusted the shelves, and drank her tea in silence. But she could not stop thinking about James Thornton and the impossible things that kept happening. She started to keep a notebook, writing down every odd event—the rose, the bookmarks, the voices, the clock message. The more she wrote, the more the coincidences connected, like pieces of a puzzle.

Still, Rachel worried about what people would think if they knew. The customers trusted her. The neighbors thought she was sensible, calm, and always polite. What if they heard she was chasing ghosts, looking for a man who might not even exist? She could almost hear the whispers—"Rachel is losing her mind." "Too many old books, too many lonely nights." But the pull was too strong. She could not just close her eyes and pretend nothing was happening.

17

One evening, Rachel sat with her best friend, Carla, at a small café. The rain tapped softly on the window as Carla sipped her coffee. Rachel wanted to share everything—the strange letters, the hidden notes, the feeling that she was living in a story written by someone else. But as soon as she began, she saw the doubt in Carla's eyes. "Are you sure you're not reading too many mystery novels, Rach?" Carla said gently. "You sound…well, a little obsessed."

Rachel blushed, feeling foolish, but she pressed on. "Carla, it's real. These things are happening. I can't explain them, but I know they mean something. I have to find out the truth."

Carla only smiled, shaking her head. "Just be careful. I don't want to see you hurt."

Rachel knew then that if she went further, she might lose her friends' trust. People might start to gossip or avoid her shop. Her reputation—her quiet, simple life—was on the line. But even with that risk, Rachel felt sure of one thing: She could not turn away from the mystery now.

That night, back in the shop, Rachel lit a candle and laid the letters out in order, determined to follow their clues wherever they led. She would visit the places James mentioned. She would talk to strangers if she had to. She would search for every clock that "stood still" in the city, no matter how strange it looked to anyone else.

Rachel closed her eyes and took a deep breath. If finding the truth meant risking everything—her peace, her friends, her good name—then so be it. She was no longer just a reader of stories. She was part of one now, and she would see it through to the end.

CHAPTER 3

The Handwritten Letters

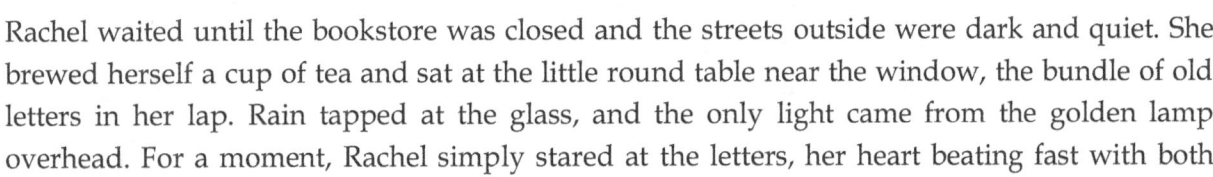

Rachel waited until the bookstore was closed and the streets outside were dark and quiet. She brewed herself a cup of tea and sat at the little round table near the window, the bundle of old letters in her lap. Rain tapped at the glass, and the only light came from the golden lamp overhead. For a moment, Rachel simply stared at the letters, her heart beating fast with both fear and hope.

She picked up the first letter. The envelope was thin and soft, almost falling apart. Inside, the paper felt delicate as a spider's web. She unfolded it slowly and began to read.

"My dearest Rachel,

I hope these words find you when you need them most. If you are holding this letter, then time itself has answered my prayers."

Rachel felt goosebumps rise on her arms. The writing was careful and beautiful, full of old-fashioned words and gentle hope. She read on:

"I have watched you from a distance—always just out of reach, but never out of my heart. Do you remember the blue lamp in your window, or the way the bookstore smells just after rain? Those are the things I love most about your world."

Rachel blinked in shock. How did he know about her lamp? The rain? She turned to the following letter, hands shaking.

"Sometimes I wish I could step through the pages and meet you where you are. For now, I must be patient. You must be brave. Trust the rose and the clocks. I will be waiting."

Each letter was signed, "Yours always, James Thornton." The words were full of longing and strange hints—references to things Rachel thought only she knew. In one letter, James described a dream she'd had as a girl: running through a field of wildflowers, calling out for someone she never saw. Rachel had never told that story to anyone. Yet here it was, written in a stranger's careful script.

19

Some letters talked about days that hadn't happened yet. One read,

"Soon, the city will be covered in white, and you will find yourself alone, but not lost. Remember, hope is a door that opens from the inside."

Rachel shivered. She looked outside at the dark street and wondered if snow was coming. The air felt cold and strange, as if something invisible had entered the room.

She read letter after letter, each one drawing her deeper into a web of mystery and memory. Sometimes she felt watched. Other times, she felt comforted, as if someone truly cared for her — someone who had been waiting for her all along.

Rachel finished the first batch and pressed them gently back into their envelopes. She realized her world had changed. These letters were not just messages; they were keys to something bigger, something she didn't yet understand.

As she turned out the lamp and climbed the stairs to her small apartment above the shop, Rachel glanced back at the letters. They seemed to glow in the dim light, waiting for her to discover their next secret.

Over the next few days, Rachel carried the letters everywhere. She slipped them into her bag before leaving home, tucked them under her pillow at night, and kept them in her apron pocket as she worked in the shop. The words written by James Thornton seemed to follow her, filling her mind with questions and a strange, growing hope.

She read the letters again and again. Each time, they touched her more deeply. The things James wrote — his memories, his longing, his gentle advice — felt like whispers only she could hear. Rachel had never been close to many people. She kept her feelings hidden, her heart safe. But these letters seemed to know her better than anyone ever had.

One morning, after a long night of reading and dreaming, Rachel sat by the shop window as the first sunlight spilled across the shelves. She opened a letter and read:

"My dear Rachel,

Even when you are alone, you are never truly lonely. Some hearts remember you, and a future is waiting for your courage. If you find yourself afraid, look for the rose and remember: love always finds a way."

Rachel's eyes filled with tears. She could feel the ache in James's words, the loneliness and hope mixed together. It was like reading a diary from someone who had lived the same pain she carried inside. For the first time in years, she let herself cry — not just for what she had lost, but for the possibility that someone, somewhere, understood.

She started to write in her own notebook again, filling the pages with her thoughts and feelings. The act of writing felt new, like she was answering James's letters in her own secret way. At night, she would whisper his name into the darkness, feeling foolish but also strangely brave.

Each letter revealed something more. James remembered details about her life she had almost forgotten: the storybook her mother read to her when she was small, the way she always counted the cracks in the sidewalk, her favorite spot in the city park. He described dreams she hadn't told anyone, and fears she kept locked deep inside. The more she read, the more she felt a connection that went beyond time or logic.

Rachel found herself waiting for signs from James. A white rose was on her doorstep. A song on the radio that matched the words in a letter. The smell of rain on old stone, just as he had written. Every sign made her heart beat faster, as if the letters had woken a part of her soul that had been sleeping.

Sometimes, the longing in James's words felt almost too much to bear. She would press her hand to her chest and close her eyes, wishing she could reach out and touch the person behind the ink and paper. The letters made her feel brave and scared all at once. She knew her life could not go back to how it was before—not now, when every word from James felt like a promise and a prayer.

And so, day by day, Rachel let herself hope. Maybe the world still held magic. Perhaps love could travel through time, written in the lines of a letter and the beating of a lonely heart.

After reading the letters so many times, Rachel began to notice small, strange things hidden in James's words. Some sentences seemed out of place, as if they were meant to stand out. She wondered if he was trying to tell her something in secret, using a code only she could break.

One rainy afternoon, Rachel sat at her kitchen table with all the letters spread before her. She read each one carefully, searching for patterns. She noticed that certain words were underlined—like "rose," "clock," and "window." In some letters, the first word of each paragraph, when put together, made a new message. In one, the hidden sentence read: "Meet me where time stands still."

Her heart raced. What did that mean? Was James asking her to go somewhere in the city? She thought of the note she had found in the green desk drawer: "Look for me where the clocks stand still." It was too much to be a coincidence.

Rachel searched the letters for more clues. She noticed that in one letter, the first letter of every line spelled out "PAST PAGES." That was the name of her bookstore. It sent chills up her spine. How could James have known to hide her shop's name in a letter written years ago?

Some clues were more mysterious. James sometimes drew small symbols in the corners of the pages—a tiny rose, a clock with its hands set to midnight, a sun half-hidden behind clouds. One letter had numbers in the margins: 12, 5, 19, 15, 6, 20. Rachel realized if she matched them to the alphabet, they spelled "L-E-S-O-F-T"—almost "LESOFT," but missing a letter. Was it another clue or just a mistake?

She decided to write all the symbols, underlined words, and odd phrases into a notebook. When she finished, Rachel saw that many clues seemed to point toward time, memory, and hidden places. She wondered if there was a real location in the city where "time stands still." Maybe an old clock tower, or a forgotten part of the park with a broken sundial.

Rachel felt both excited and nervous. The letters had become a puzzle she was determined to solve. But the more she found, the more she wondered who James really was. Was he from the past—or somehow watching her now? Was he playing a clever game, or was he truly reaching out through time?

She stayed up late that night, matching clues, looking at old city maps, and searching online for places where clocks had stopped or were famous for being stuck at midnight. The mystery pulled her in, making her forget about everything else.

As Rachel drifted off to sleep with the letters beside her, she dreamed of ticking clocks, roses falling through the air, and a man waiting in the shadows. She woke before dawn, sure of one thing: the clues were real, and she would follow them wherever they led—even if it meant stepping into the unknown.

Every night, after locking up the bookstore and making sure the windows were shut against the wind, Rachel would settle into her favorite chair by the window. The city was quiet at that hour, just the distant hum of traffic and the soft glow of streetlights. It was the only time Rachel truly felt safe enough to open her heart.

She would place James's letters in her lap, choosing one at random to read again. The paper always felt cool and thin, almost like it might vanish if she held it too tightly. Sometimes, she would light a candle or make a cup of tea, letting the gentle warmth calm her nerves. In those moments, surrounded by shadows and the faint scent of old books, Rachel felt less alone.

Her nightly ritual became a kind of comfort—a bridge between her world and the strange, impossible world James described in his letters. She liked to imagine him sitting somewhere, far away or long ago, writing to her by candlelight, just as she was reading by it now. She wondered if he could sense her hope or hear her whispers in the dark.

Rachel began to keep a small notebook by her side, where she would write her thoughts after reading a letter. Some nights, she scribbled questions:

Who are you, James?

How do you know so much about me?

Are you real—or am I dreaming all of this?

Other times, her words were softer—confessions of loneliness, memories of her mother, or fears she could never share with anyone else. The more she wrote, the more it felt like she was talking to James, answering his letters in her own secret way.

On certain nights, the lines between her memories and James's words blurred. She would read a sentence and suddenly remember the day her mother gave her the blue lamp, or the time she ran through the rain with a book tucked under her coat. It was as if James's letters could open hidden doors in her mind—places she thought she'd forgotten.

Rachel sometimes read aloud, her voice trembling but steady. She would close her eyes and listen to her own words, hoping the sound might reach James, wherever or whenever-he—he was.

"If you can hear me," she whispered once, "I believe you. I want to find you."

She wondered if she was losing her grip on reality, letting herself become too wrapped up in old stories and faded ink. But every morning, when she woke with the letters beside her, she felt a new strength, as if James's words were guiding her through each day.

As the weeks passed, Rachel's nightly rituals became a secret she cherished. They gave her comfort and courage, even as the mystery deepened. She promised herself she would never stop searching for answers, and every night she would keep reading, hoping that, one day, the letters would finally reveal the truth—and maybe, just maybe, lead her to James himself.

On a quiet night, after reading another of James's letters, Rachel leaned back in her chair and closed her eyes. The words she'd just read lingered in her mind:

"When the world feels too heavy and the days are cold, remember you are never alone, not really. There is always someone listening, somewhere."

Rachel felt a strange ache in her chest, and memories began to stir—memories she tried not to visit too often. She saw herself as a little girl, standing at the window of her mother's tiny apartment, watching as raindrops slid down the glass. The apartment always felt too big when her mother worked late. Rachel would count the lights in the building across the street, wishing for someone to talk to, someone to fill the quiet.

After her mother died, the silence became even deeper. Rachel remembered sitting at her aunt's kitchen table, listening to the tick of the old clock and trying not to cry. She had a book clutched in her hands, reading the same paragraph over and over, just to feel close to someone, anyone, who understood. Even then, stories were her comfort. Sometimes, she would imagine that a kind voice was reading along with her, telling her not to give up.

23

As she grew older, the loneliness didn't leave; it just changed shape. Rachel remembered sitting in the corner of the school library, watching the other kids laugh and talk, afraid to join in. She always felt like a shadow at the edge of the crowd, safe only when she had a book to hide behind.

James's letters seemed to reach out and touch these quiet places inside her—the places where she was still that lonely child, wishing for a friend. Sometimes, a line in his letter would bring back a memory so sharp it almost hurt.

"You are stronger than you think," he wrote. "Even on the darkest night, your light shines."

Rachel thought of the night she moved into her own apartment for the first time. She was so proud and so scared, surrounded by boxes and dust, afraid of the emptiness. That first night, she had cried herself to sleep. If only she had known, even then, that someday someone would write her letters, someone who seemed to know every hope and fear she carried.

She realized, with a shiver, that James's words were not just comfort—they were a mirror. They showed her the person she tried to hide, and made her feel seen in a way no one else ever had. Sometimes, it felt as if James had watched her life from afar, leaving gentle messages for every time she stumbled.

As Rachel opened her eyes and looked at the letters spread across her lap, she wiped away a tear. The loneliness wasn't gone, but it didn't feel so heavy anymore. There was someone, even if only in words, who understood what it meant to be lost and alone—and who kept reaching out, across time, to remind her that hope was still possible.

CHAPTER 4

Curiosity Awakens

———— ·∞· ————

The more Rachel read James's letters, the deeper her obsession became. She could not stop thinking about the strange details, the clues, and the hidden messages. Each letter pulled her in further, making her hunger for answers she couldn't yet find.

Rachel stopped noticing the days passing. She let the phone ring without answering, left meals half-finished, and lost track of time. The bookstore was still open, but her mind was always elsewhere, trapped in the puzzle of James's words. Her dreams were filled with roses, ticking clocks, and distant voices calling her name.

Every morning, Rachel woke early and went straight to her desk, notebooks and letters spread out before her. She filled page after page with notes: places mentioned in the letters, dates and times, coded words, and drawings of the strange symbols James had left. The letters now felt like maps, leading her somewhere just out of reach.

Rachel pored over city maps, old newspaper clippings, and public records. She visited the library again and again, searching for stories about clock towers, mysterious disappearances, or people named James Thornton. Her eyes grew tired from reading, but she pressed on, fueled by a need she could not explain.

She also searched the internet late into the night, clicking through history websites, online forums, and digital archives. Sometimes she found hints—a photograph of an old clock in the city square, or a story about a white rose left on a stranger's doorstep—but never anything that thoroughly explained the mystery. Every small discovery led to more questions, like stepping into a maze that kept changing around her.

Rachel even started to notice changes in herself. She hardly spoke to her friends or neighbors anymore, worried they wouldn't understand her obsession. Her sleep became restless, full of dreams that felt too real. She was no longer just reading letters—she was living inside their world.

On her days off, Rachel walked around the city, looking for places James had mentioned. She visited the opera house, the park, the bakery, and every clock she could find. She wrote down the times shown on the clock faces, searching for patterns. Once, at the old clock tower, she saw a rose placed carefully on a windowsill. It made her heart race—was it another sign from James, or just her imagination?

The more Rachel learned, the more she needed to know. She became convinced that the answer was close, just out of sight. Sometimes, she worried that she was losing herself, slipping too far into a story with no clear ending. But every time she considered stopping, she would read another letter, and the longing in James's words would pull her back in.

Rachel knew she was changing. She felt braver, even as fear pressed at the edges of her thoughts. If she could solve the mystery, maybe she would finally understand why James had chosen her, and what secret waited for her at the end of his letters.

Rachel sat at the bookstore counter, her notebook open and filled with scribbled dates, places, and strange phrases from James's letters. She tapped her pen against the paper, thinking hard. She had read each letter so many times that the words danced in her mind, but now she needed proof that the things James described were real—and not just the wild hopes of her lonely heart.

She started by listing all the places James had mentioned: the old opera house on Fifth Avenue, the bakery with honey cakes, the city park with the iron bench, and, of course, the clock tower where time "stood still." Then she compared these to her own memories and searched the local news online for stories that matched.

The opera house was easy. James had written about the night it would glow with new lights, and, to Rachel's amazement, that night had happened last spring—the same night she had walked by and noticed how the building seemed almost magical in the rain. She found a newspaper article with a picture that matched James's words exactly. That gave her hope.

Next, Rachel thought about the bakery. James's letter described the owner, Mrs. Flores, and her golden bell, which made a soft sound whenever someone walked through the door. Rachel went to the bakery herself. Mrs. Flores smiled as she rang up Rachel's order. When Rachel asked about the bell, Mrs. Flores laughed and said, "That bell's been there since I opened the shop. My father gave it to me." It felt like a small sign, something only someone very close—or from another time—would know.

At the city park, Rachel found the iron bench under the tall old oak tree, just as James had described. She ran her fingers along the carved initials in the wood, searching for a clue. There was nothing unusual at first, but then she found a tiny rose petal pressed between the cracks. Her heart fluttered. She took it as another secret message.

Some clues were more challenging to check. James had written about a heavy snowfall that would trap Rachel inside her shop for a day. That hadn't happened yet, but winter was coming, and Rachel began to watch the weather more closely.

26

Rachel even visited the old clock tower. She stood at the base and looked up at the huge clock face, its hands stuck at midnight, just as James had written. She took a photo and compared it to a drawing in one of his letters—they matched perfectly. At that moment, Rachel felt a mix of excitement and fear. If all these things were true, then James's letters were not just stories. They were messages from someone who knew her world better than she did.

As she left the tower, Rachel realized the line between reality and the mystery was starting to blur. Her early attempts to connect the letters with real events had changed everything. It meant that James, whoever he was, was honest—or that something impossible was happening. And with every step, Rachel felt herself pulled deeper into the story, no longer able to turn back.

Rachel knew she couldn't keep the mystery to herself forever. The letters, the clues, and the strange coincidences were growing too big for one person to handle. She needed someone who would listen without laughing or thinking she had lost her mind. After much thought, she decided to visit Dr. Westfield, her favorite professor from university, who still worked at the city's history museum.

She made her way through the gray, rainy streets to the museum, holding the oldest letter in her pocket. Her heart beat faster with every step. What if Dr. Westfield didn't believe her? Or worse, what if he thought she was making everything up?

When she arrived, the old professor was sitting behind his desk, surrounded by towers of books and old photographs. He looked up with a warm smile when he saw Rachel. "Well, if it isn't my brightest student," he said, motioning for her to sit.

Rachel smiled shyly and sat across from him. For a moment, she hesitated, turning the letter over and over in her hands. "Dr. Westfield," she began, her voice soft, "I need your help. But you have to promise not to think I'm...well, a little crazy."

He laughed gently. "You always did have the most interesting questions. Go on, Rachel. I'm listening."

Slowly, Rachel told him everything—the package, the letters from James Thornton, the hidden clues, and the strange things that had begun to happen in her life. As she spoke, she watched his face for any sign of disbelief, but Dr. Westfield only grew more interested. When she handed him the letter, he held it up to the light, squinting at the neat, slanted handwriting.

"This is beautiful," he said. "It looks like it was written with a fountain pen. And this paper... Rachel, it's at least fifty years old. Where did you say you got it?"

She explained about the mysterious package left at the shop. Dr. Westfield nodded thoughtfully. "And this James Thornton—do you know anything about him?"

Rachel shook her head. "Nothing. I've searched everywhere. He mentions things that haven't happened, and things about my life no one should know."

Dr. Westfield leaned forward, his eyes kind. "Sometimes, history hides in plain sight. Sometimes, the best stories are the ones no one believes at first." He smiled. "Let's not rush to explain it away. People have always hoped to reach across time, to leave a mark, to connect."

Rachel felt a wave of relief. He wasn't laughing or telling her to stop. He believed she was telling the truth.

"I'll help you look into this, if you want," Dr. Westfield said. "Let's study the handwriting, the ink, the clues. And Rachel, trust your instincts. There's more to the world than what we can see."

Rachel left the museum that afternoon with new hope and a lighter heart. For the first time, she felt like she wasn't alone in her search. With Dr. Westfield's help, she was ready to dig even deeper into the mystery, no matter where it might lead.

Back at the museum, Rachel and Dr. Westfield spread the letters out on a long table, careful not to damage the fragile paper. Outside, rain tapped gently against the tall windows, turning the afternoon gray and quiet. The strange words, clues, and hidden messages filled the space between them, pressing for answers.

Dr. Westfield leaned back in his chair and looked at Rachel. "Let's think about this together," he said kindly. "We have letters dated from the past, talking about things that happened just recently or haven't happened yet. The handwriting matches, and some clues seem too perfect to be random. How do we explain it?"

Rachel hesitated. She felt nervous saying her wildest thoughts out loud. "I keep asking myself the same thing," she admitted. "Sometimes I wonder... is it possible that James is a time traveler? Maybe he really has seen the future—my future. It sounds crazy, I know, but nothing else fits."

Dr. Westfield smiled. "History is full of stories about messages sent across time. People have always dreamed about it—secret codes, letters in bottles, lost diaries. Time travel is a popular idea for a reason. But we should look for other answers too."

Rachel nodded, fiddling with the edge of a letter. "I also thought about reincarnation. Maybe I had another life, and James did too. Maybe we're connected in some way, and the letters are a way for his old self to reach me now."

"That's another idea," the professor agreed. "Reincarnation, soulmates, people meant to find each other across lifetimes. Many cultures believe in it." He pointed to one of the letters. "This line about remembering things you shouldn't know—like the blue lamp, or the garden—could fit that theory."

Rachel's voice grew soft. "But then, there's always the chance it's just a very clever trick. Someone could have researched me online, found out details, and written these letters as a kind of game or…a literary prank."

Dr. Westfield considered this. "Yes. Maybe someone with too much time on their hands, or a writer wanting to see how you'd react. But it would take a lot of planning and care. These letters are so old, and the paper and ink seem genuine."

Rachel sighed, torn between hope and doubt. "I want to believe it's real. That someone is reaching out from another time, or another life. But what if I'm just letting my dreams get the better of me?"

Dr. Westfield smiled gently. "That's the thing about mysteries, Rachel. Sometimes, you have to follow the story, even if it sounds impossible. The answers might not be what you expect, but the journey will always teach you something new."

Rachel stared at the letters, her mind swirling with theories. Time travel, reincarnation, a prank—or maybe something else she hadn't thought of yet. Whatever the truth was, she felt closer to it than ever before.

With Dr. Westfield's help, Rachel knew she would keep searching, no matter how strange the story became.

After the talk with Dr. Westfield, Rachel tried to see the world with open eyes. She told herself to stay careful, to keep questioning every clue, but the strange things happening around her made it harder to hold on to her doubts.

One morning, Rachel walked into "Past Pages" to find every clock in the shop—three old wall clocks and the tiny gold one on her desk-all stopped at exactly twelve o'clock. She checked their batteries, shook them gently, even wound the little gold clock, but nothing worked. It was as if time itself had chosen to pause in her bookstore. Goosebumps prickled her arms. She remembered James's clue: "Meet me where time stands still."

That same afternoon, she was sorting through a box of donated books when she found a novel she had lost years ago. It was her childhood favorite, and she hadn't seen it since she was twelve. On the inside cover, in neat handwriting, was a new message:

"For Rachel—hope is never lost."

She touched the words, heart pounding. The handwriting was just like James's.

29

A few days later, Rachel closed up the shop early to visit the old clock tower downtown. As she walked, it began to snow. The flakes grew thick and heavy, covering the streets in a white blanket. She watched as the city slowed, then stopped, cars silent and people huddled indoors. By the time she reached the tower, the streets were empty—she was alone in a world of white and stillness, just as James had described in his letter.

When Rachel went home, she found a white rose waiting on her doorstep, wrapped in a blue ribbon. There was no card, no sign of who had left it, just the gentle scent of the rose filling the cold air. She stood in the doorway, shivering, her mind racing. Was someone watching her? Or was James somehow reaching through time, leaving her these small miracles?

More odd things happened. Once, she opened a book to find her own name hidden in the text—something she had never noticed before. Another time, the radio in her kitchen turned on by itself and played a song that James had mentioned in one of his letters, a song she hadn't heard since her mother was alive.

Rachel's skepticism wavered. She wanted to believe there was a logical explanation for every strange event. But the pattern was too strong, too personal. Every miracle felt like a whisper in her ear, telling her to trust what she could not see.

At night, Rachel sat in her window with James's letters, watching the snow fall and the city lights blur. She whispered, "If you're real, please give me another sign."

And the wind seemed to answer, rattling the windows softly—almost like a promise.

Rachel's world had always been quiet and safe. Now, every day was filled with new wonder, making her believe that sometimes, the impossible really could happen. The miracles were small, but together, they changed everything.

CHAPTER 5

James Thornton's Time-Traveling Adventures

Long before the letters found Rachel, James Thornton lived a life filled with secrets he could never share. As a young man, James felt out of place, always watching the world with curious eyes. He loved old things—clocks, letters, faded photographs—anything that held the feeling of another time.

One rainy afternoon, when James was barely twenty, he found himself wandering through an old antique shop at the edge of the city. The air smelled of dust and forgotten stories. His fingers traced the curves of a heavy silver pocket watch sitting on a high shelf. It was beautiful, with tiny roses engraved on the back and a crack in the glass face. The old shopkeeper smiled when he saw James staring at it.

"That one's special," the man whispered. "They say it holds more than just the hour."

James bought the watch, drawn to it for reasons he couldn't explain. That night, at home, he wound the watch and listened to the soft ticking as rain pattered against his window. The room grew quiet. Suddenly, the ticking stopped, even though the watch was still running in his hand.

James felt dizzy. He looked around and noticed the street outside had changed. Instead of the usual city lights and car horns, he saw horse-drawn carriages and gas lamps. He hurried outside, his heart pounding, and realized the whole city looked different—older, quieter, and touched with a strange kind of magic.

Afraid and amazed, James wandered the streets. No one seemed to notice him as he moved past them, almost like a ghost. He looked down at the pocket watch. The hands had stopped at midnight. When he pressed the stem again, the world seemed to spin, and suddenly everything returned to normal. James was back in his own time, the rain still tapping at his window.

For days, James tried to make sense of what had happened. Was it a dream, or had he really traveled through time? He tested the watch again, each time feeling the dizzy pull and finding himself in another year—sometimes in the future, sometimes in the past. Each trip lasted only a short while, but the feeling stayed with him long after he returned.

31

James kept his secret close, too afraid to tell anyone. The pocket watch became his most precious thing, a doorway to all the times he could never live. He learned to use it carefully, leaving small clues and gentle notes for those who might need them, never changing history, only watching and waiting.

But in every year, in every place, one thing always pulled at James's heart: the hope of finding someone who felt as lost as he did. Someone who believed in things unseen. It was this hope that led him to Rachel—a name he began to see everywhere, a face that haunted his dreams.

The night James first wrote a letter to her, he promised himself that if anyone could believe in the impossible, it would be her. And so, with every letter sent and every trip through time, James searched for Rachel, hoping she would find his words and follow them, no matter how far across the years he had to reach.

At first, James felt wonder every time the pocket watch whisked him into another year. He wandered through old streets, watched celebrations and quiet moments, and stood in awe as history unfolded around him. Each time, he promised himself he would be careful, never to touch, never to change, only to watch.

But soon, the wonder gave way to something heavier. James saw tragedies before they became headlines—fires, floods, heartbreak, and wars. He saw people he could never save and happiness he could never share. The rules of time were clear: to step lightly and leave no mark. The pocket watch always pulled him back if he tried to change even the smallest thing.

Once, he tried to warn a woman about an accident that would happen the next day. He slipped her a note, but when he returned, he saw that fate had simply changed its shape. She had avoided one danger only to meet another. James felt the weight of guilt pressing on his heart. He realized he was only meant to watch, never to guide.

He saw children playing in the streets, unaware of the hard times coming for their families. He stood in silent crowds during parades and protests, longing to join in but always apart. Sometimes, he visited years that were lonely and empty, the city lost in silence and sadness. He wrote down what he saw in little notebooks, filling page after page with memories that no one else would ever know.

James felt invisible, caught between worlds. No one remembered him from visit to visit. He wanted so badly to reach out and change someone's story for the better. But every time he tried, the world shifted back, erasing any trace of his kindness. The pocket watch was both a gift and a prison.

There were nights when James could not sleep, haunted by all he had seen. He thought of the faces of strangers—those who laughed, those who cried, those who disappeared too soon. Their stories stayed with him, pressed into his heart like the petals of a rose. He wondered if anyone would ever know how much he cared.

32

The only thing that made the loneliness bearable was his hope for Rachel. Every year, he searched for her—a sign, a letter, a memory waiting for him to find. Sometimes he thought he saw her from a distance: a girl with bright hair and thoughtful eyes, a woman sitting quietly by a window, a name scribbled in the margin of a forgotten book. But the rules held him back, always just out of reach.

James wished he could shout into the world, tell someone everything he knew. But he kept his silence, carrying the burden of history alone. He poured his longing and love into letters, hoping they would find Rachel and that, somehow, she would understand what it meant to watch the world and never truly belong.

And in the quiet moments, when the weight became too much, James would open the pocket watch, close his eyes, and whisper a silent promise: "I will find you, Rachel. Even if I can never change the past, I will leave you every hope I have."

James walked through centuries like a shadow, passing through crowds and families, always watching but never joining in. Each time the pocket watch pulled him into another year, he felt the same ache—a longing for someone to notice him, to say his name and remind him he was real.

At first, James tried to fill the emptiness with small comforts. He wrote notes in the margins of library books, hoping someone, someday, would find his words. He left pressed roses between the pages, drew little clocks in the corners of old newspapers, and sometimes whispered "hello" to strangers who would never remember his face. But these small acts were never enough. When he returned to his own time, the world had moved on without him.

James's loneliness grew deeper each year. He watched couples dancing in candlelight and families sharing meals by the fire. He saw friends laughing together and children running through fields. It was always the little moments that hurt the most—the touch of a hand, a gentle smile, a voice calling out in the night. James wanted to belong, but the rules of time kept him apart, locked behind an invisible wall.

He spent many nights staring at the stars, his only companions the ticking of the pocket watch and the letters he wrote to Rachel. Sometimes, he imagined what it would be like to sit across from her in a warm room, to share stories and secrets and dreams. The thought made him smile, but it also brought tears to his eyes.

The letters became his only way to reach out, to send a part of himself across the distance that separated them. He poured his hopes and fears onto the page, telling Rachel things he had never told anyone. He wrote about the moments that made him happy and the sadness that would not let him go. He hoped, with every word, that she would understand—that she would know he was more than just a stranger from another time.

33

There were days when James wondered if he should stop. Maybe the letters would never reach her. Perhaps he was only making things more complicated for himself. But then, he would remember the first time he saw her name—written in the flyleaf of an old book, a name that called to him like a promise. That hope, fragile and bright, kept him going.

His longing for connection was more than just wanting to be seen. James wanted someone to honestly know him, to share in the joy and pain of his strange life. He wished for a friend, a confidant, maybe even love—someone who could help carry the weight of all he had witnessed.

So he kept writing, kept watching, and kept hoping. Every time he traveled, every time he left a clue, James whispered a silent plea: "Find me, Rachel. Please, find me."

And somewhere in his heart, he believed that one day, his words would be enough to bridge the distance between them, and he would finally belong.

One autumn evening, while creeping through a year-long past, James found himself drawn to a small city street he'd never walked before. The air was cool and filled with the smell of rain and wood smoke. People hurried by with their coats pulled tight, their faces lost in thought. James watched from the edge of the sidewalk, invisible to all.

He carried his pocket watch in his hand, fingers nervously brushing its silver surface. He had learned to let his instincts guide him, following feelings he couldn't explain. That night, something in his chest tugged him toward a bright window on the corner—light pouring out onto the wet pavement.

Inside, a young woman sat in a cozy bookstore, curled up in a green chair with a book resting in her lap. The sign above the door read "Past Pages." James's breath caught in his throat. He felt an instant, powerful pull—like a thread had just tied itself from his heart to hers.

The woman was reading, her hair shining in the lamplight, a small smile on her lips. Every so often, she would look up and gaze out the window, as if searching for something just beyond her reach. She looked both lonely and hopeful, a quiet dreamer lost in her own world.

James pressed closer to the glass, keeping himself hidden in the shadows. He watched as she closed her book, stood, and moved through the shelves with gentle care, running her fingers along the old spines. He saw the way she stopped at a row of rare books, pausing to straighten a volume as if it mattered deeply to her.

His heart raced. He wanted to step inside, to introduce himself, to ask her about the stories she loved and the life she lived. But he couldn't. He was out of place, a visitor from another year. If he tried to cross the threshold, the pocket watch might pull him away, snapping the thread before it had a chance to form.

Still, James couldn't leave. He watched as the woman—Rachel, he learned from the shop sign— made tea and turned on a blue lamp in the window. The soft light glowed through the night, a beacon calling him home. He wondered if she felt the same strange sense of being watched, if she could feel the air in the room grow warmer with the weight of his gaze.

Before he left, James pressed his hand gently against the cold glass, wishing she could see him. He promised himself he would return, again and again, until he found a way to reach her. As the world shifted and the sounds of the city changed, James's final glimpse was of Rachel reading by the lamplight, surrounded by books and dreams.

That night, as he wrote his first letter to her, James knew for sure: Rachel was the person he had searched for across all his lonely years. And from that moment on, every journey through time would carry her name in his heart.

After seeing Rachel through the bookstore window, James could not get her out of his mind. Each time he traveled through time, his steps seemed to lead him back to her street, to the warm glow of "Past Pages." He watched her from afar, arranging books, serving tea to customers, sometimes just sitting quietly with a faraway look in her eyes.

He felt her loneliness. He saw how she smiled at people but kept her heart tucked safely away. James knew the feeling well. He wondered what she dreamed about and if she also wished, late at night, for someone to understand her.

One evening, back in his small apartment crowded with notebooks and clocks, James paced the floor. The longing to reach out to Rachel grew stronger with each passing day. He wanted to tell her she wasn't alone—that someone, somewhere, knew her story and cared. But the rules of time weighed on him. He had never dared to make direct contact before. Was it right to break the silence now?

He sat at his desk and opened a drawer full of fountain pens and heavy paper. The air in the room seemed to thicken, charged with hope and fear. James stared at the blank page for a long time, the words tangled in his mind. Finally, he took a deep breath and began to write:

"My dearest Rachel,

If you are reading this, then time itself has been kind to us. I hope these words reach you when you need them most…"

As his pen moved, the loneliness in his heart poured out onto the paper. He wrote of the things he had seen: the blue lamp glowing in her window, the soft hush of her shop after closing time, the way she lingered among the rare books as if searching for magic. He wrote about his own story, too—never the whole truth, but enough for her to know that he understood what it meant to be different, to carry sorrow, to hope for more.

35

James hesitated, pen hovering above the page. What if this was a mistake? What if the letters never found her, or if they only made things more complicated for both of them? But he knew, deep inside, that he could not stay silent. If he could not join her in her world, he could at least send her a piece of his own.

He finished the first letter and signed it, "Yours always, James Thornton." Then he wrote another, and another, each one filled with hidden clues and secret wishes — words that might guide her, comfort her, or simply remind her that she mattered.

That night, James packed the letters carefully, wrapped them in old ribbon, and prepared to leave them where he knew Rachel would one day find them. As he set the final letter aside, he felt a quiet hope. Maybe the letters would bridge the distance between them. Maybe, across the impossible period, she would read his words and know, at last, that she was not alone.

CHAPTER 6

The Growing Connection

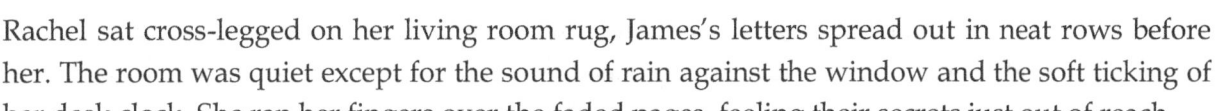

Rachel sat cross-legged on her living room rug, James's letters spread out in neat rows before her. The room was quiet except for the sound of rain against the window and the soft ticking of her desk clock. She ran her fingers over the faded pages, feeling their secrets just out of reach.

It had been weeks since she first received the mysterious package, and the letters had become her whole world. Each time she read them, she noticed something new—a word that stood out, a line that didn't quite fit, a tiny symbol drawn in the margin. She couldn't shake the feeling that James was guiding her, leaving a trail of breadcrumbs through time.

One evening, while rereading a letter about the opera house, Rachel's eyes landed on several words that were underlined: "clock," "rose," "window," "midnight." At first, they seemed random, but when she looked at the other letters, she saw the exact words appearing again and again. She began to circle them in red pen.

Rachel grabbed her notebook and wrote down all the underlined words from every letter. Soon, she spotted a pattern. The words lined up to form simple instructions:

"Go to the clock tower at midnight. Bring the rose."

Her heart hammered in her chest. She flipped through the letters, searching for more. In the corners of several pages, she noticed numbers—sometimes written as times, sometimes as dates. She matched them to places James had described. For the first time, she realized he was telling her exactly where to go and when.

Excitement surged through her. She pulled out the old city map she kept in her drawer and marked each location mentioned in the letters. The opera house, the city park, the bakery with the golden bell, and the clock tower where "time stands still." She traced a path between them and saw they formed a rough circle, with her bookstore right at the center.

Rachel laughed nervously. Was it possible? Was James giving her a treasure hunt—a way to reach him, or maybe to discover the truth behind the letters?

37

She stayed up late that night, reading the letters by candlelight. She wrote down every symbol and strange phrase she found, determined not to miss a single clue. She noticed that some lines in the letters, when read together, formed messages only she could understand:

"You are closer than you think."

"Trust your heart, and follow the signs."

"Where the rose meets the clock, the truth waits."

The more she decoded, the stronger the connection felt between them. It was as if James was speaking directly to her, reaching across time and space to guide her every step.

Rachel made a plan. Tomorrow night, she would follow James's instructions and go to the clock tower at midnight, the pressed rose hidden in her coat pocket. She didn't know what she would find, but she knew she had to try.

For the first time, she felt both afraid and thrilled. The letters were no longer just words — they were a map, a promise, and a call to adventure she couldn't ignore.

Rachel barely slept the night before her first real journey. When morning came, she packed the letters, her notebook, and the pressed rose in her bag. The sky was overcast, and the city streets were still wet from last night's rain. As she walked out the door, her heart raced with both fear and excitement.

Her first stop was the bakery James had described — the one with honey cakes and the golden bell. Rachel had been there before, but this time it felt different. She stood outside the door for a moment, staring at the tiny bell hanging above her head. When she pushed the door open, the bell chimed softly, just as James had written. The scent of warm bread and sugar filled the air. For a split second, Rachel felt as if she'd lived this exact moment before. She saw Mrs. Flores behind the counter, just as James described, and it was almost like watching a scene from a dream she'd forgotten.

Next, Rachel walked to the city park. She wandered among the old trees and quiet paths, searching for the iron bench under the tall oak. When she found it, her breath caught. The bench was exactly as James had described — dark green, with a small heart carved into the wood. Rachel sat down and looked up at the spreading branches, feeling another wave of déjà vu. She remembered reading here as a child, even though she hadn't thought of it in years. Was it just a memory, or was James helping her remember forgotten parts of her own story?

The afternoon grew chilly as Rachel made her way to the opera house. Its tall stone columns and wide steps loomed above the street. She stopped at the base of the steps and stared up, seeing the building through James's eyes. The new lights shone on the front entrance, just as his letter had promised. As people hurried past, Rachel felt strangely apart, like she was moving through layers of time, connected to both the present and the past.

Her final stop was the clock tower. The sun was setting as Rachel climbed the hill and stood beneath the giant, silent clock face. The hands were frozen at midnight, just like in the letters. For a moment, the world seemed to grow still. Rachel closed her eyes and let the silence surround her. She imagined James standing here, looking up at the same clock, writing her secret messages in the night.

Everywhere she went, Rachel felt a strange tug inside—a mix of memory and mystery. She saw familiar sights as if for the first time, and unfamiliar places that felt oddly close to her heart. The sense of déjà vu grew stronger, as if her life and James's had been intertwined all along.

As dusk fell and the city lights flickered on, Rachel walked home, her mind spinning with questions. Was she following James's path, or was he following hers? With each step, the lines between past and present blurred, and Rachel knew her journey was only just beginning.

After she visited the places in James's letters, Rachel's dreams began to change. At first, they were soft and hazy—just colors and feelings drifting through her sleep. But soon, the dreams became vivid, so real that Rachel sometimes woke with her heart pounding, unsure if she was still dreaming.

In her dreams, she often found herself walking through old city streets at night. The lamplight glowed golden on the wet pavement. She could hear the distant ticking of clocks and the gentle chime of a bell. Sometimes, she saw a man with kind eyes and a silver pocket watch, standing in the shadows. He always seemed just out of reach. Whenever Rachel tried to speak, the words caught in her throat.

Other times, the dreams felt like memories that didn't belong to her. She saw through someone else's eyes—riding in a horse-drawn carriage, stepping inside a candlelit bookstore, or sitting at a desk covered in fountain pens and yellowed paper. In those moments, Rachel felt a deep sense of longing, a hope that someone, somewhere, would answer the letters waiting on the desk.

One night, Rachel dreamed she was inside the old clock tower. The air was thick with dust, and the giant gears groaned softly as they turned. She saw the frozen clock face and reached out to touch the minute hand. As soon as her fingers brushed the cold metal, the world seemed to tilt. She heard a voice—a gentle whisper: "Rachel, I am waiting. Find me where time stands still." She woke with a start, her heart hammering, the words echoing in her ears.

The dreams were not always comforting. Sometimes they left Rachel shaken and lonely, unsure of what was real. Once, she dreamed of standing in the rain with a white rose in her hand. She turned, and for a split second, she saw James's face—kind, tired, and full of longing. He reached out to her, but before their hands could meet, she woke up, tears on her cheeks.

39

Rachel wondered if these dreams were only in her imagination or if James was dreaming of her, too. Some mornings, she wrote down every detail she could remember, hoping the clues would help her understand. Once, she woke to find a new letter on her desk that she didn't remember opening the night before. It spoke of a dream in which James saw her sitting beneath the old oak tree in the park, reading by the golden light of sunset. The words matched her own dream exactly.

The line between dreams and waking life blurred more each day. Rachel began to feel that her connection with James was growing stronger, as if their thoughts and memories could reach across the walls of time. Each night, she waited for the dreams to come, hoping for a sign, a message, or even just the touch of James's hand.

And in the quiet moments before dawn, when the world was still and the city slept, Rachel whispered into the darkness, "I see you, too," hoping somehow, somewhere, James could hear her.

It was almost midnight when Rachel left her apartment, clutching the pressed rose and James's latest letter. The city was quiet under a cloudy sky. She walked quickly, drawn by a feeling she couldn't explain, toward the old clock tower—just as the hidden instructions had said.

The streets were empty, except for the soft splash of her footsteps on wet pavement. Rachel's breath came in little clouds as she hurried up the steps of the tower, her heart beating wildly. She paused, hand on the old wooden door, and listened. Somewhere above, a clock chimed once—midnight.

Inside, the air was cold and smelled of old stone and dust. Rachel's footsteps echoed as she made her way up the spiral staircase. At the top, moonlight poured through the glass, casting strange shadows across the floor. She stared up at the great clock face, frozen at twelve.

Rachel stood still, hugging her coat tighter. "James?" she whispered into the darkness, not sure if she really believed he could hear.

For a moment, there was only silence. Then, she felt a sudden shift in the air—a tingling along her skin, like electricity before a storm. She spun around and gasped.

In the far corner of the room stood a man, half-hidden in shadow. He wore an old-fashioned coat and held a silver pocket watch in his hand. Rachel couldn't see his face clearly, but something about him felt achingly familiar.

Her mouth went dry. "James?" she said again, her voice trembling.

The man stepped forward, and for a split second, Rachel saw his eyes—kind, full of sorrow, and somehow full of hope. He smiled gently, and Rachel felt a strange warmth rush through her.

"I've waited so long to meet you," he whispered, voice barely above the wind. "Thank you for following the signs."

Rachel stepped closer, holding out the rose, but as she moved, the air seemed to shimmer. For a heartbeat, it felt as if the world paused, like the clock overhead. Rachel could almost feel James's hand brush hers, cold and soft, before he began to fade.

"No, wait—don't go!" she cried, reaching for him. But he was already slipping away, the outlines of his coat and face dissolving like mist in the moonlight.

"I'm sorry," he said, his voice growing faint. "We don't have much time… but I will find you again. Follow your heart, Rachel."

Then, just as suddenly as he had appeared, James was gone. The air grew still, and the only sound was Rachel's own heartbeat echoing in the tower.

She stood in the empty room, the pressed rose shaking in her hand, trying to understand if what she had seen was real. Tears filled her eyes, but she was not afraid. She felt a strange hope—the certainty that, somehow, their story was not over.

As she walked home through the quiet city, Rachel knew she would keep searching, no matter how impossible it seemed. The mystery was alive, and now, so was she.

The night after Rachel's encounter in the clock tower, she couldn't sleep. She lay in bed, staring at the ceiling, replaying every second of what she had seen. The image of James—his gentle eyes, his sad smile—wouldn't leave her mind. The feeling of his presence still clung to her, both comforting and unsettling.

But as dawn crept through her curtains, doubt began to slip in. Had she really seen James? Or had the loneliness and the letters finally pushed her too far? She sat up, hugging her knees to her chest, her heart pounding with fear and confusion.

Rachel's days began to blur together. Sometimes she would find herself standing in the middle of the shop, unable to remember why she had walked there. She spoke to customers but couldn't recall their faces. When she tried to talk to Carla or Dr. Westfield, she struggled to explain what was happening. The words got stuck in her throat, and she felt foolish, like a child telling ghost stories no one believed.

Was she dreaming? Was the clock tower meeting real, or had she imagined it out of longing and exhaustion? Rachel checked the rose in her coat pocket, just to be sure. It was still there, soft and fragile as ever. She ran her fingers over James's letters, searching for proof that she wasn't making it all up.

But the signs kept coming. She found new notes in the green desk drawer, messages that hadn't been there before. She heard James's name whispered in the sound of the radio, saw his

41

handwriting on scraps of paper she didn't remember writing. At times, Rachel felt like the world itself was twisting around her, changing shape every time she tried to look closer.

She grew afraid to tell anyone what she was experiencing. What if they thought she needed help, or worse, that she had lost her mind? Rachel started to doubt herself. She wondered if the pain of her past—her mother's loss, her years of loneliness-had finally become too much to bear. Was she inventing this mystery to fill the emptiness inside her?

One afternoon, as she closed the shop and watched the rain pour down outside, Rachel pressed her forehead against the glass and let herself cry. The city seemed so far away, the people outside rushing through lives she could never be part of.

But even through her tears, Rachel could not let go of the hope James had given her. His letters were real. The clues and the feelings they stirred inside her were too sharp to be a dream. Somewhere, she believed, there was truth beneath the madness.

With a trembling hand, Rachel wrote in her notebook:

"I don't know if I'm losing my mind. But if I am, I want to see this mystery through to the end. I want to believe that love and time can still work miracles—even if only for me."

As she wiped her eyes, Rachel felt a small spark of strength. She didn't know where the journey would lead, or if she would ever find James again. But she knew she had to keep going, no matter what the world—or her own mind—told her.

CHAPTER 7

James' Forbidden Love

James sat at his desk, staring at the pocket watch that ruled his strange life. The room was filled with ticking clocks he had collected from every era he'd visited. But none gave him peace. With each journey, he felt the rules of time tighten around him, silent but heavy.

He wanted nothing more than to reach out to Rachel, to save her from loneliness, to change small things for the better. But the warnings haunted him. In the past, every time he had tried to interfere with the world around him, something went wrong. The pocket watch would pull him away, or the future would twist itself, leaving him with guilt and fear.

James remembered the time he slipped a note to a child about to run into the street. The child stopped—but later, James saw that the same child got hurt another way. Time did not like being changed. It fixed itself, sometimes cruelly. He learned that every act of kindness could bring pain somewhere else.

He also worried about Rachel. If he changed her path, what would happen? Would she become someone different—someone who no longer believed in magic, or never opened the shop where he first saw her? The risk was too significant. Still, the longing to help her grew stronger each day.

There were rules he had to follow, rules that whispered in his mind whenever he tried to get too close:

You can leave clues, but not answers.

You can watch, but not touch.

You must never steal a moment that belongs to someone else.

James tried to stay strong, leaving only gentle hints—pressed roses, messages hidden in books, lines in letters that Rachel alone would understand. But sometimes, as he watched her struggle with loneliness, he felt the urge to step out of the shadows and take her hand, to change fate just this once.

One night, after visiting the clock tower, James wrote a letter he never meant to send.

"My dearest Rachel,

There are things I wish I could give you—time, comfort, answers. But every change I make ripples into your world in ways I cannot control. I am so sorry for every sorrow I cannot stop. Know that even from afar, I am with you. Yours, always."

James held the letter to his heart, feeling the weight of his choices. He wondered if Rachel would ever forgive him for being so close and yet so far away. He asked if the day would come when he had to make an impossible choice—protect her by leaving her alone, or risk everything to reach her.

The rules of time felt like chains, keeping him apart from the one person who made his lonely existence matter. But James would keep searching for a way to help, to love, and maybe—just maybe—to break the rules, if it meant saving Rachel's heart.

And as he wound the pocket watch for his next journey, he promised himself that he would keep trying, even if the cost was everything.

There were some things James never wrote in his letters to Rachel. He kept them hidden, locked deep in his heart. The truth was, she wasn't the first person he had tried to reach across time. Before Rachel, there were others—faces blurred by years and memories shaped by sorrow.

He remembered a girl named Evelyn, from a city street lit by gas lamps and laughter. She was bright and fearless, with a voice that carried through crowded rooms. James had watched her fall in love, then watched as fate took her from the world too soon. He tried to help, slipping a warning note beneath her door, hoping to change the smallest thing. But the note vanished, and so did Evelyn—gone in a way that left James aching for years.

There was Samuel, a friend James made during one winter in the past. Samuel was kind and curious, always asking questions about the stars. James wanted to tell him everything, to share his secret gift. But the rules of time held his tongue. When Samuel grew sick, James tried to leave medicine where Samuel might find it. Still, nothing changed. Samuel's life ended quietly, a page turned too soon.

Once, in a bustling city far away, James met a woman named Elise. She was gentle, a librarian who loved rare books almost as much as Rachel. For a time, James let himself believe he could belong there—with her, in that quiet world of stories and candlelight. But one night, the pocket watch pulled him away before he could say goodbye. When he returned years later, Elise was gone, and the library stood empty.

Each time, James learned that time did not like to be touched. Fate was stubborn. Trying to save someone always led to heartbreak. The world twisted around his kindness, leaving him with only memories and regrets.

These tragedies taught James to be careful, to watch and listen, but never interfere. The pain of each loss shaped him, making his heart both softer and more guarded. He carried their names like secret scars, never speaking them aloud.

Still, he hoped. With every failed love, every goodbye, he kept looking for the one person who might change everything. Someone who could see him, not as a ghost or a stranger, but as a man lost between moments, searching for connection.

When James first saw Rachel through the bookstore window, something felt different. The loneliness inside him eased, just a little. He thought of all the people he had lost, the tragedies he had witnessed, and wondered if this time would be different. If fate had finally led him to someone who could break through the walls of time.

James never wrote about these past loves or heartbreaks in his letters to Rachel. He wanted her to see only hope and possibility, not the shadows that trailed behind him. But every word he wrote was shaped by those memories—the longing, the pain, and the hope that this time, love might finally find a way.

James sat in a candlelit room, surrounded by clocks of every shape and age. The air felt heavy, thick with the secrets of time. As he watched the shadows flicker along the walls, he remembered the first time he met the guardians—the silent men and women who moved between years like ghosts, watching those who dared to bend the rules.

He had been young then, still learning what it meant to travel through time. His mentor, a gentle man named Mr. Alder, had found him wandering lost in a strange year. Mr. Alder taught James how to listen to the language of clocks, how to slip through moments without leaving a trace, and how to resist the urge to change what was meant to be.

"Time is like a river," Mr. Alder said, his voice low and kind. "You can float along its current, but if you try to dam it, the water will find another way. You can watch, you can learn, but you must never change its course."

James listened, but as he grew older and lonelier, the warnings grew sharper. Sometimes, when he returned from a journey, he would find a note on his table, written in careful script: "You are being watched." Other times, he felt the presence of the guardians—a sudden chill, a shadow moving where there should be none.

One evening, after James left a rose for Rachel in her shop, the air around him grew cold. He turned and saw a woman standing in the doorway, dressed in old-fashioned black, her eyes steady and sad.

45

"James Thornton," she said quietly, "you are tempting fate. You know the rules."

James swallowed hard. "She's lonely. She deserves hope. I only want to help."

The woman shook her head. "Every gift you give has a price. Every change echoes through the years you cannot see. You cannot know the damage your kindness might cause. If you care for her, let her live her story. Don't steal a moment that isn't yours to touch."

James's chest tightened. He wanted to argue, to tell her about the sorrow he'd seen, the pain he wished he could erase. But he knew the guardians were right. He had seen what happened when he tried to alter fate—tragedies twisted, stories broken, love lost in the shifting currents of time.

Before she left, the woman offered one last warning. "Remember, James: If you cross the line, you may lose more than you can bear. Some travelers disappear. Some are forgotten by everyone, even those they love. Time has a way of correcting itself—and sometimes, it erases those who try too hard to help."

James watched her vanish into the shadows, the room growing silent once more. He sat with his hands trembling, staring at the pocket watch in his lap. He wanted to reach out to Rachel, to change just one thing, but now he knew the risks.

Haunted by the guardians' warnings, James promised himself to be careful. Still, the longing in his heart burned brighter than ever. He would try to follow the rules, but deep down, he wondered if love was worth any consequence.

James sat at his small desk, a fresh letter to Rachel half-written in front of him. The candle flickered, casting long shadows on the walls, as he stared down at the words. His hand trembled above the page, pen frozen mid-sentence. For the first time since he began writing, James did not know how to go on.

He thought of the guardians' warnings—their voices still echoing in his ears. "If you cross the line, you may lose more than you can bear." The threat of being erased, of hurting Rachel, pressed heavily on his chest. Every letter was a risk. Every clue could change the future in ways he could not see.

But the longing in James's heart would not let him rest. Each day without Rachel felt colder and lonelier. He remembered the first moment he saw her in the glow of the bookstore lamp, the hope that flared inside him, the belief that he had finally found someone who might understand his strange, drifting life.

He lifted the letter, reading what he had written. He wanted to tell Rachel everything—to share his secret, to promise her that she was not alone. But with every truth he shared, he feared the damage he might do. Would the letters help her or only lead her further from her own life? Was it fair to pull her into his world of shadows and impossible dreams?

James pressed his hand to his eyes, trying to block out the memories of all the times he had tried to change fate before. The tragedies, the losses, the faces of those he could not save. He knew the cost of crossing time's boundaries. He knew he could lose Rachel forever.

Yet, when he thought of stopping—of leaving her in silence, never sending another word—the pain was almost unbearable. The thought of Rachel alone, wondering and hoping for answers that never came, was worse than any punishment time could give him.

James's heart ached with the choice before him. If he stopped writing, maybe he could keep her safe. Perhaps the guardians would let him stay, a silent witness, forever on the edge of her life. But if he risked everything—if he sent the following letter, if he tried to meet her one last time—he might lose his place in the world, or worse, lead her into danger.

He stared out the window at the silent city. Somewhere, Rachel was waiting, searching for him, hoping for another clue. James wanted to believe that love was stronger than the rules of time. He wanted to trust that their story could have a happy ending, no matter the cost.

At last, with tears in his eyes, James picked up his pen. He would not give up—not yet. For Rachel, he would risk it all. He finished the letter, sealing it with a pressed rose and a silent promise:

"I will find you. No matter the price, no matter the consequence, I will not stop searching for you."

James stared at his latest letter to Rachel, the ink still wet on the page. All night, he had wrestled with the warnings of the guardians and the ache of his own heart. He knew the rules—he was supposed to be careful, to watch but not change, to leave only gentle hints. But those days felt over now. Rachel was closer than ever, searching for him with a courage that took his breath away.

He read her last response, the lines trembling with hope and confusion:

"I'm following your clues, but I need more. Please help me understand. I want to find you."

James pressed his fist to his heart. He knew what he wanted to do. If the guardians erased him for it, at least he would know he had tried. He reached for his notebook, flipping through the pages of notes and city maps he had kept for years. This time, he would not just leave quiet messages—he would show Rachel exactly where to look.

He wrote in careful, hidden code, using the language and symbols she had already learned to see.

"Find the place where roses bloom out of season, where the clock's chime is heard only by those who wait after midnight."

He included a drawing of the old city greenhouse, its windows covered in climbing roses, and marked a secret door in the back. He wrote of a statue in the park that Rachel had passed a hundred times, but never noticed the number etched on its base—12:03, a minute past midnight, the very moment the watch first stopped for him.

Each clue he gave was more direct, more dangerous. The guardians would notice if Rachel got too close to the truth. But James could not turn away now. He felt as if time itself was pushing them together, giving him one last chance to reach her.

He wrote another letter, this time tucking a key between the pages.

"This opens a box beneath the city's oldest clock. Inside is the truth you seek, Rachel. But be careful—once you open it, everything may change."

As he sealed the letter and pressed a white rose inside, James's hands shook with both fear and hope. He whispered into the candlelit room, "Forgive me if I'm wrong. I want you to find me, even if it means breaking every rule I've ever known."

He left the letters where he knew Rachel would find them—places tied to their shared memories and dreams. As he did, the air around him grew colder, and he felt, for the first time, the eyes of the guardians watching closely.

Still, James would not stop. He had made his choice. If love meant risking everything—his freedom, his memories, his very place in the world—then that was the price he would pay.

As he walked away from the clock tower that night, James whispered into the shadows, "Come find me, Rachel. I'm waiting, no matter the cost."

CHAPTER 8

Following the Clues

Rachel could hardly believe the boldness of James's latest clues. The letters were more direct now, with exact times, places, and hidden codes that sent a shiver of both excitement and fear through her. She felt the stakes rising with every word. Still, her longing for answers was stronger than her worry.

She packed a small bag with James's letters, her notebook, a flashlight, and the delicate key he had left for her. She tucked the pressed white rose inside her coat pocket and set out into the city, her heart pounding. The night air was cool and sharp, full of promise and danger.

Her first stop was the old city greenhouse, hidden in a forgotten corner of the park. Rachel slipped through a rusty side gate and walked among the tangled vines and overgrown roses. She searched the place as the moonlight poured through broken glass, following the directions in James's letter. At the back, she found the secret door—just as he had drawn—and opened it. Inside, a small tin box waited on a shelf. With trembling hands, Rachel opened it and found a slip of paper:

"Look for the statue who keeps time after midnight."

She hurried on, following the clues as the city grew quiet. At the statue in the park, Rachel brushed away leaves until she found the numbers James described: 12:03. She checked under the statue's base and found another message taped there, this one in a familiar, careful script:

"The truth waits beneath the oldest clock. Use the key. Be brave."

Rachel moved quickly, crossing empty streets and silent squares. Her mind raced as she reached the old clock tower, heart in her throat. She let herself inside, climbed the winding staircase, and searched until she found a small, rusted box bolted beneath the giant clock's mechanism.

With shaking fingers, Rachel fit the key into the lock. It turned with a soft click. Inside the box was a folded letter, older than the rest, with James's handwriting covering both sides. The words trembled with urgency:

49

"Rachel, this is all I can give you. What you do next will change everything. If you choose to follow, I will be waiting where time and memory meet."

As she read, Rachel felt as if the whole city was holding its breath. The world around her seemed to pause, the city lights blurring and the wind whispering through the clock tower. She wondered if the guardians James had written about were watching, if she was really prepared for whatever came next.

But there was no turning back now. Each clue, each discovery, made her feel more alive than she had in years. The fear was real, but so was her hope. Rachel tucked the final letter into her coat, took a steadying breath, and looked out over the city, ready for the last step in the treasure hunt, wherever it might lead.

She whispered, "I'm coming, James. I won't stop until I find you."

As Rachel followed each clue through the city, it became clear that the treasure hunt was more than just a game. Every hidden message and secret place felt like a window into James's world—and into parts of her own heart she had never seen so clearly before.

At the greenhouse, when Rachel stepped through the secret door, she found an old photograph tucked behind a pot of wild roses. It showed a young man—James—standing outside the very same greenhouse, holding a notebook and looking quietly determined. On the back, he had written,

"Every beginning is just another chance to hope."

Rachel stared at the photo, feeling a strange wave of connection. She realized that James had visited these places long before her. They shared the same sense of wonder, the same longing to believe that magic could be real. For the first time, Rachel wondered if her own dreams had called James to her, just as much as his longing had drawn her.

At the statue in the park, Rachel found an envelope taped beneath the base. Inside was a page from an old book—a story about a lonely child who learned to be brave by following secret signs in the world around her. Rachel recognized herself in every line. At the bottom, James had written,

"You are braver than you think, Rachel. You've always had the strength to find your way."

Rachel pressed her hand to her chest, blinking back tears. All her life, she had doubted her courage, hiding in stories and quiet places. But each clue proved she was capable of more than she believed. It was as if James saw her better than anyone ever had.

At the clock tower, as she unlocked the rusted box, she found another treasure: a small pocket watch, nearly identical to the one she had seen James carry in her dreams. Tucked inside was a final letter. In it, James revealed something he had never told her before—his fear of being forgotten, his loneliness in a world where he could only watch, never belong.

"I see you, Rachel," the letter read. "Even when you feel invisible, you are not alone. You have given me hope when I had none left. If I have broken the rules, it was for you. If I disappear, remember that our story is proof that love can cross any distance – even time."

As Rachel held the watch in her hand, she felt her own fear and loneliness begin to melt away. She realized she was not just solving a mystery—she was changing, becoming braver, more open, more willing to risk her heart.

Every clue was a gift, not just from James but from herself—a reminder that she was worthy of love, of adventure, and of being seen. She understood now that the real treasure was not in the letters or the clues, but in the person she was becoming on the journey.

Rachel took a deep breath, pocketed the watch, and stepped out of the tower, ready for whatever the next revelation would bring. She was no longer afraid. She was finally ready to meet James, no matter what waited at the end of the story.

Rachel's search through the city didn't go unnoticed. Along her path, she met people who would shape her journey in ways she never expected.

Her first challenge came from Carla, her oldest friend. When Rachel told her about the treasure hunt and the clues left by James, Carla frowned. "Rach, you're chasing shadows," she said, shaking her head. "All these late nights, strange places... I'm worried about you. What if it's just a trick, or worse, someone trying to hurt you?" Carla's concern made Rachel pause. For a moment, she wondered if she was being foolish, letting hope blind her to danger. But the memories and clues were too real to ignore. Rachel promised Carla she'd be careful, though inside, she knew she had to keep going.

At the greenhouse, Rachel was startled by an older woman watering the roses. Instead of sending her away, the woman smiled kindly and asked if she was lost. Rachel hesitated but decided to trust her. To Rachel's surprise, the woman listened with patient interest as she described the letters and clues. "I believe in stories that choose us," she said softly, handing Rachel a small rose cutting. "Sometimes the right people are guided to the right places." The stranger's quiet faith gave Rachel new courage. She pressed the rose cutting between the pages of her notebook as a sign she wasn't alone.

In the city park, while searching for the statue at midnight, Rachel met a young man with sharp eyes and a nervous manner. He watched her as she checked the numbers on the statue and glanced around, as if expecting someone else to appear.

"You're not the only one looking," he said quietly, surprising Rachel. "Others want to know the truth about the clock tower and the letters. Not all of them mean you well."

Rachel tensed, gripping her bag tightly. "Who are you?" she asked.

He just shrugged. "A rival, I guess. Some people think the letters are valuable or magical. Be careful who you trust, Rachel. Not everyone wants you to finish this story." Before Rachel could ask more, he slipped away into the shadows, leaving her uneasy and alert.

Even as doubts and danger crept in, Rachel found support from strangers along the way. A librarian at the city archives offered to help her search for records about James Thornton, sliding her a list of old addresses and newspaper clippings. The night watchman at the clock tower let her inside after hours, simply nodding at her when she showed him the old key. "Sometimes, you just know when someone's on an important journey," he said, holding the door open.

For every person who doubted her, there was someone who understood—someone who believed, even if only for a moment, in the magic of Rachel's quest.

These encounters—both helpful and suspicious—reminded Rachel that she was not the only one changed by this mystery. She had to trust her instincts, lean on those who wished her well, and watch out for those who wanted to keep the truth hidden.

With each new friend, warning, and act of kindness, Rachel felt herself growing stronger, her hope lighting the way through even the darkest parts of the city.

Late one evening, as Rachel continued her search through the city, she returned to the quiet park where so many clues had led her before. The air was cool and full of the sound of leaves rustling in the wind. She followed the path past the statue, the iron bench, and the old oak tree, letting her feet guide her in the pale light of the street lamps.

James's letters had hinted at something real, something she could hold—a promise that their story was more than just words. Tonight, she felt closer than ever to the answer.

Rachel stopped at the far end of the park, beside a small stone fountain James had described in one of his letters:

"Under the stone where the water first falls, you'll find a piece of me waiting for you."

Her heart pounded as she knelt by the fountain. She reached beneath the edge, fingers brushing against cold stone, searching for anything that felt out of place. For a moment, nothing happened. Doubt crept in. Was this just another wild hope, another trick of her lonely heart?

Then her hand closed around something small and hard. She pulled it free, gasping softly as moonlight glinted off the surface. It was a silver pocket watch, old and beautifully crafted, its surface engraved with tiny roses and the initials "J.T."

Rachel turned the watch over and over in her hands, hardly daring to believe it was real. The metal was cold and heavy. She pressed the stem, and the watch sprang open. Inside, instead of a ticking clock face, was a folded slip of paper.

With shaking fingers, Rachel unfolded the note. In James's careful handwriting, it read:

"My dearest Rachel,

If you are holding this, then you know our worlds have truly touched. This watch is the bridge between us. I have carried it across the years, hoping one day you would find it. Trust in what you feel. Time cannot keep us apart forever.

Yours always,

James."

Tears filled Rachel's eyes as she read the message. This was proof—something real, something that could not be explained away by dreams or tricks of memory. She closed her hand around the watch, feeling the weight of James's hope and love.

For a long time, Rachel sat on the cold stone, staring at the pocket watch. The night seemed full of promise, as if the world had opened just for her. She remembered all the moments of Doubt, all the warnings and whispers, and realized none of it mattered now.

James had found a way to reach her—not just with words, but with something she could hold and keep. Rachel tucked the watch carefully into her pocket and stood, stronger than before. She would keep following the clues, keep trusting her heart.

With each step, the line between past and present blurred a little more, and Rachel knew—no matter what happened next—she was not alone in her journey.

The silver pocket watch felt warm in Rachel's hand as she reread James's final letter, searching for the meaning hidden in his words.

"When the clock strikes midnight and roses bloom out of season, follow the music to the place where stories begin and end. There you will find me — at the Blooming of the Timeless Rose."

Rachel's heart pounded with hope and fear. She had never heard of such an event, but the letter was clear: this was the moment everything would change.

She walked the city streets, searching for signs. Posters fluttered on lamp posts, some new, some faded. Her eyes caught on one she'd never seen before—a simple design: a silver pocket watch, surrounded by roses, with bold letters beneath:

THE BLOOMING OF THE TIMELESS ROSE

Midnight, Past Pages Bookstore

Rachel's breath caught. The bookstore — her own sanctuary — was to be the center of the story. She hurried home, the city seeming to glow around her, filled with a strange and secret energy. The closer midnight came, the more the air shimmered, as if time itself was holding its breath.

Inside Past Pages, everything felt different. The lamps burned brighter, casting golden halos over the old shelves. Rachel placed the silver watch on the counter, her heart fluttering with every tick, every second drawing her closer to the truth.

Just before midnight, the bell over the door chimed softly, though Rachel hadn't seen anyone come in. Music floated through the shop — a gentle melody, somehow both familiar and new. Rachel followed the sound, weaving between shelves until she reached the old reading nook where she had spent so many lonely nights.

There, in the center of the room, stood a rosebush she had never seen before. White roses bloomed thick and full, glowing in the lamplight, though it was the dead of winter and no roses should have survived the cold. At the heart of the bush, nestled among petals, rested another pocket watch — twin to the one James had left in the park.

Rachel reached out, her fingers trembling. As she touched the watch, the world seemed to pause. The clocks in the shop stopped ticking. The music grew louder, swirling around her as the air grew warm and sweet with the scent of roses.

A voice spoke softly — James's voice — echoing in the stillness: "Rachel, you found me. Time has kept us apart, but love found a way."

Rachel closed her eyes, tears slipping down her cheeks. For a moment, she felt James beside her — a gentle presence, both near and far, as if he had stepped out of the story and into her life.

The roses glowed brighter, and the bookstore seemed to fade, replaced by a light that felt like the beginning of a new dream. Rachel clutched the pocket watch, whispering, "I'm here, James. I never stopped believing."

As the clock struck midnight, the Blooming of the Timeless Rose reached its peak. Time bent, and the impossible became real. Rachel knew her journey had brought her home, not just to James, but to herself, changed and full of hope.

CHAPTER 9

The Intertwined Destinies

As midnight echoed through the bookstore, Rachel stood surrounded by the blooming roses, the twin pocket watches pressed tightly in her hands. The golden lamplight flickered, shadows dancing across the shelves as the music swelled and seemed to fill every corner of the room. Time itself felt stretched—each second sweet and heavy, as if the world was waiting for something miraculous.

Rachel closed her eyes, breathing in the scent of the roses and listening to her heartbeat. She felt the energy shift, like a warm breeze brushing her skin. Suddenly, the music faded, and the silence grew deep and soft.

She opened her eyes, and James was standing before her.

He looked exactly as she had seen him in dreams and glimpses: gentle eyes, a kind smile, his coat dusted with the magic of countless journeys. In his hand, he held his own pocket watch, the chain glowing faintly in the light.

For a moment, neither of them spoke. Rachel was afraid that if she moved or blinked, he might disappear. But James stepped forward, his eyes shining with hope and awe.

"Rachel," he whispered, as if tasting the sound of her name for the first time. "You found me."

Tears filled her eyes. "I never gave up. I followed every clue, even when I was scared. I had to believe you were real."

James smiled, a warmth spreading through the room. "You were my hope, too. Through every year, every letter, I waited for this moment. I wasn't sure it was possible—but love can bend any rule, even the rules of time."

Rachel reached out, half expecting her hand to pass through him like a dream. But his fingers met hers, warm and genuine. In that touch, all her doubts faded away. The clocks had stopped, the guardians were silent, and for the first time, the distance between them vanished.

55

They stood together among the roses as midnight's magic settled over them. For the first time, Rachel felt fully seen, fully known. She could feel the ache of James's loneliness, the hope in his letters, the strength it took for both of them to keep believing.

"I don't know what comes next," Rachel whispered, resting her head on his shoulder.

James wrapped his arms around her, steady and sure. "Neither do I. Maybe time will push us apart again. Maybe we only have this night. But even if the world tries to erase us, I'll never stop loving you. We've already proven that stories—our story—can change everything."

Rachel smiled through her tears. "We're here now. That's enough."

For a while, they stood in the golden lamplight, surrounded by roses, the only sound the gentle ticking of two pocket watches beating in perfect time.

In that moment, Rachel and James knew they had bent the rules of the world for love. No matter what waited beyond midnight, their hearts—and their story—would always find a way back to each other.

As Rachel and James held each other, the world around them began to shimmer and shift. The golden lamplight flickered, growing brighter, then softer, as if the air itself was turning into light. The walls of the bookstore seemed to breathe, the shelves bending and stretching, their outlines fading in and out.

Rachel blinked, heart pounding. She felt as if she was standing in two places at once. Behind her, she could hear the familiar sounds of "Past Pages"—the creak of the floorboards, the distant hum of the city at night. But layered over those sounds came something new: the song of birds she had never heard before, the clip-clop of horse-drawn carriages, voices speaking in old-fashioned tones.

James squeezed her hand gently, his eyes wide with wonder. "Do you feel it?" he whispered. "It's like we're between worlds—between the past and now."

Rachel nodded, too awestruck to speak. She looked down at the pocket watches in their hands, noticing how the second hands ticked forward, then backward, sometimes pausing completely. Each time the watches stilled, the room would blur, and for a heartbeat, she glimpsed a different reality.

One moment, she stood in the bookstore, surrounded by books and roses; the next, she was in a grand old library, golden sunlight pouring through stained glass, rows of ancient clocks ticking on the walls. She saw herself as a little girl, reading in the park with her mother. Then she was James, gazing through a rain-streaked window at a world that was just out of reach.

The air felt charged—alive with stories and memories layered on top of each other. Rachel could feel the weight of every moment they had both lived, and the hopes they still carried. It was as if time itself had broken open, pouring out everything they had ever loved or lost.

For a few shining minutes, Rachel and James walked through these shifting worlds together. They saw old friends, lost loves, and guardians standing watch in the shadows. Rachel touched the spines of books that glowed with secrets. James listened to the heartbeat of the city, feeling both joy and sorrow.

Neither of them knew how long the magic would last. The edges of the world shimmered like water, sometimes clear, sometimes cloudy. It was dizzying and wonderful, like a dream they didn't want to wake from.

But through it all, they stayed side by side. Rachel realized that no matter what reality they stood in, her hand found James's, steady and sure.

As the midnight hour stretched thin, Rachel felt a gentle sadness. She sensed the magic beginning to fade, the worlds sliding back into their places. She pressed her head to James's chest, listening to the twin ticking of their watches.

"If this is just a moment," she whispered, "I'm glad I shared it with you."

James kissed her hair, his voice soft. "Even between worlds, we found each other. That's more than I ever hoped for."

And as the shifting worlds grew still, Rachel and James held on, knowing that, whatever reality they woke up to, the bond between them would never be broken.

As the shifting of the world slowed and the glow faded from the air, Rachel and James found themselves once again in the heart of the bookstore. The roses drooped quietly, the pocket watches lay still in their hands, and the city outside seemed silent and waiting.

For a long moment, neither spoke. They simply stood together, holding on tightly, afraid that even a breath might break the fragile spell that still lingered around them. But soon, a cold draft crept through the shop, and with it came a feeling Rachel had felt only once before—the presence of something watching, something not quite human.

James's face grew troubled. He pulled Rachel closer and whispered, "The guardians. They know what we've done."

Rachel's heart squeezed with fear. She looked around, half-expecting to see shadows gathering in the corners. "What will they do to us?"

James swallowed hard. "They warned me, Rachel. Breaking the rules—bringing two worlds together—always comes with a price. I don't know what it will be, but I'm scared. Not for myself. For you."

At that moment, the golden light in the room flickered and grew colder. A tall figure stepped out from the shadows behind the counter—a guardian, dressed in black, her eyes shining with ancient sadness.

"You have crossed the boundaries of time," the guardian said, her voice echoing softly. "Such love is powerful, but it leaves scars on the world. What is gained can be lost. What is changed may never return to how it was."

Rachel stepped forward, shaking but determined. "Please—don't take him from me. We've come so far. We didn't mean to break anything. We just wanted to be together."

The guardian regarded her with pity and a hint of warmth. "Love is a miracle and a danger. You have shown great courage, Rachel. But all magic demands balance. You must both choose: accept the memories and heartbreak that come with breaking time's laws, or let go, and allow the world to heal without you together."

James reached for Rachel's hand, his eyes filled with longing and regret. "Whatever happens, I want you to remember me. I want you to be safe, even if it means losing everything else."

Rachel shook her head, tears shining in her eyes. "I don't want to forget, James. Not any of it. Even if it hurts, I want to remember our story—the love, the hope, the impossible night."

The guardian nodded. "So be it. Your memories will be your blessing and your burden. The world may not understand, but you will always have this night, this love, and this truth."

The air grew warmer again, and the guardian faded back into the shadows, leaving Rachel and James alone, changed forever.

Rachel pressed her forehead to James's, whispering, "We faced the consequences. We chose each other."

James smiled, a mix of relief and sorrow on his face. "Whatever comes next, we did it together."

As dawn crept across the city, Rachel knew life would never be easy, but their story—beautiful, painful, and real—was finally, truly theirs.

As the first pale light of dawn crept through the bookstore windows, Rachel and James sat together on the old reading bench, surrounded by fallen rose petals and the soft ticking of their pocket watches. For the first time, there were no more secrets between them. The magic of the night had faded, but a deeper kind of closeness remained.

Rachel turned to James, searching his face for the man she had met in dreams and glimpses. She reached for his hand and squeezed it gently. "Tell me everything," she whispered. "Not just the beautiful parts, but the hard ones too. I want to know the real you."

James took a long breath and nodded. He spoke quietly, his words slow and careful. He told her about his strange gift—how he had stumbled into time-travel by accident, how he had learned to watch but never touch, and how each journey left him more alone. He spoke of the friends and loves he had lost along the way, of the heartbreaks that lingered long after time pulled him away. His voice broke when he described the guilt he felt for every moment he could not save.

Rachel listened, her eyes shining with tears. She shared her own story in return—her childhood with her mother, the pain of her mother's death, the years of feeling lost and invisible. She told James about her love for stories and the way books became her only home, how she had built a life inside the walls of Past Pages because it was the one place she felt safe. "I always hoped for something more," she said softly, "but I never believed it could really happen. Not until you."

They sat in silence for a moment, just breathing and holding hands. The pain they shared felt lighter now, less sharp. The air between them was full of understanding—a gentle acceptance of all the scars and stories that had brought them here.

James looked at Rachel and smiled through his tears. "Even when I was alone, I hoped someone would find me. I never stopped believing in you, not even when the world tried to keep us apart."

Rachel leaned against his shoulder, feeling the warmth of his arm around her. "We can't change the past, James. But we can choose what we do now. I want to live every moment, even if we don't know how much time we have."

A new hope blossomed in their hearts. They knew there would still be sadness and fear ahead. The world might never understand their story, and the guardians' warnings would always echo in the shadows. But in that quiet morning light, surrounded by books, roses, and each other, Rachel and James found a peace they had never known.

Their pain became the soil for something beautiful to grow. Their hope was the promise of a future they would shape together—one day at a time, one heartbeat, one memory, one shared story after another.

As the morning sun climbed higher, golden light filled the bookstore, painting the shelves and the floor with warmth. Rachel and James sat side by side, still holding hands, both feeling a sense of peace that went beyond words. The chaos of the night—the magic, the shifting worlds, the warnings of the guardians—seemed to settle, leaving only the quiet truth between them.

Rachel brushed her hair behind her ear and turned to James. "Do you ever wonder," she asked softly, "if all of this was meant to be? If we were supposed to find each other?"

James nodded, his gaze steady and full of tenderness. "I've felt it since the first time I saw you. There was always something about you that pulled me in—something I could never explain. Even before I wrote the letters, your name would appear in old books, in stories I read across the years. Sometimes I felt like I was searching for you long before I even knew who you were."

Rachel's heart beat faster. She thought of all the moments she had felt different—of all the dreams, the flashes of déjà vu, the stories that seemed to whisper her name. She remembered the first time she held one of James's letters, the sense of belonging she felt, as if some invisible thread had finally pulled her home.

"We were always reaching for each other," Rachel said quietly. "All those years I spent feeling alone, wishing for someone to understand… maybe you were out there, wishing the same thing. Maybe all the little things that made me feel lost were really just signs pointing me to you."

James smiled, his eyes shining. "And every place I visited, every time I felt like a ghost, it all led me here to you. Maybe it wasn't just luck or magic—maybe it was destiny. Maybe we're part of a story that's been waiting to be told for a very long time."

Rachel felt tears well up in her eyes, but they were happy tears—tears that washed away the last of her doubts. She squeezed James's hand and leaned her head against his shoulder, closing her eyes and letting herself believe.

In that moment, everything made sense. The letters, the dreams, the clues, and miracles—each one was a piece of a puzzle that only fit because their destinies were entwined. They saw it in the twin pocket watches ticking softly together, in the roses blooming in winter, in the comfort they found just being together.

Their connection was bigger than time, bigger than fear. It was written in every heartbeat, every hope, every quiet promise to keep searching no matter what. Rachel and James knew that, whatever came next, they had already won something rare and wonderful—the discovery that they were never truly alone.

Hand in hand, they looked out at the morning light, grateful and amazed that all along, fate had been gently guiding them to this very moment.

CHAPTER 10

James' Final Leap

For a little while, it seemed as though Rachel and James had finally found peace together. The guardians kept their distance, the magic of the night faded into soft morning light, and hope filled the small bookstore. But underneath it all, James felt the weight of a terrible choice pressing on his heart.

He had broken the rules to be with Rachel. Each moment they spent together made the world's edges blur a little more. He could feel time twisting—strange cracks in memories, brief flashes where the shop was empty or Rachel's face flickered like a half-remembered dream. The pocket watch in his hand sometimes stuttered, skipping seconds or stopping altogether. The guardians' warning echoed in his mind: "Every change has a cost. If you go too far, the world will fix itself… and erase the one who caused the break."

James watched Rachel as she shelved books and laughed at some small joke. Her happiness lit up the room, and he knew with a sharp ache that he would do anything to protect her—even if it meant losing everything.

One evening, as the sun dipped behind the city skyline, James saw a shadow moving at the edge of the shop. The same guardian woman from before stood there, silent and watching.

"You know what you must do," she whispered, her voice carrying both sorrow and sternness. "Time is unraveling. The cracks will soon become a storm. Rachel's fate is tied to yours now, but only you can pay the price to set things right."

James's throat tightened. "If I erase myself, will she be safe? Will she remember?"

"She will live," the guardian said gently, "and the world will heal. She may remember, or she may not—but her heart will be whole again. If you stay, both of you may be lost to the storm."

James looked back at Rachel, feeling tears burn in his eyes. Was this the end of their story? He wanted to fight, to find another way, but every instinct told him there was no other path. He walked over and took Rachel's hands in his own, feeling the warmth and hope between them.

"I have to go," he whispered, his voice shaking. "If I stay, everything we have—everything you are—might be lost forever. I can't risk you, Rachel."

"No!" Rachel cried, clutching his hands tighter. "We just found each other. There has to be another way. Please, James…"

James pressed his forehead to hers, letting the tears fall. "You saved me. You made me real. I will always love you, no matter what happens."

As the world around them shimmered, James made his decision. He kissed Rachel softly and let go of her hands. The room filled with golden light, and for a moment, all the clocks ticked in perfect time.

"I'll find you again," he promised, as his form began to fade, "in this life or the next."

Rachel reached for him, but her arms closed on empty air. The light dimmed, and the shop fell silent once more.

James was gone.

As the golden light swallowed him and his form faded from the world, James felt memories rush over him—sharper, clearer, and more painful than ever before. He was no longer in the bookstore with Rachel, but drifting through the moments that had defined his life.

He saw himself as a younger man, stepping through the rain in a year long past. There was another woman at his side then—Evelyn, with laughing eyes and a brave heart. He remembered the joy of loving her, the quiet talks by candlelight, the dreams they shared for a future he knew he could never have. He also recalled the moment he let her go. Evelyn had fallen ill, her fate already written. James wanted desperately to save her. He tried, bending every rule, leaving medicine and warnings, risking the wrath of the guardians. But the more he struggled, the more the world pushed back. In the end, Evelyn slipped away, her last smile full of forgiveness. James had to watch her vanish, knowing his love could not change her fate.

Another memory surfaced: a boy named Samuel, a friend James had made in the early days of his travels. Samuel was kind and endlessly curious, always asking about the stars and the secrets of the universe. James knew that if he revealed his gift, Samuel's life would change forever—maybe for the worse. So James kept silent, sacrificing the friendship they might have had to keep Samuel safe. Years later, he learned that Samuel died young, never knowing what his friend truly was.

Every sacrifice cut a little deeper, each one leaving its mark. But the pain of losing Rachel was worse than anything that came before. With her, James had believed—just for a moment—that he could rewrite the rules, that love could defeat loneliness and longing. He had risked everything to bring them together, but now the price had come due.

62

Floating between worlds, James saw Rachel's face—her courage, her tears, her laughter. He saw the way she looked at him, the way she held his letters to her heart, believing even when she was afraid. He had given her all he could: clues, hope, love, and a piece of himself.

The guardians' words echoed in the emptiness: "Every change has a cost." James had always known, deep down, that his fate would be to love from afar and to let go for the sake of another's happiness.

But even as he faded, he clung to hope. He had touched Rachel's life and made her believe. She was stronger now, braver, ready to face the world with or without him. That was what mattered most.

James whispered into the emptiness, "It was worth it—all the pain, all the years. I would choose you every time."

And as the last pieces of his existence drifted away, James held on to one final promise: that love, even if it must be sacrificed, never truly disappears. It lingers, like a story waiting for its next chapter.

As James's presence faded from Rachel's world, the atmosphere inside the bookstore grew strange. The air turned cold, the lamplight shivered, and the silence deepened into something almost alive. Rachel stood motionless, clutching the silver pocket watch to her chest, grief and confusion battling in her heart.

Suddenly, the bell above the shop door rang, though no one had entered. Shadows gathered at the edges of the room. Three figures stepped from the darkness—the guardians, their forms half-seen, their eyes old and full of sadness. They moved silently, their footsteps making no sound on the wooden floor.

Rachel backed away, frightened but defiant. "Why are you here? What do you want from us?" Her voice trembled, but she refused to look away.

The woman guardian who had once spoken to James stepped forward, her face both kind and stern. "We are not here to punish you, Rachel," she said quietly. "But balance must be restored. The lines between worlds have blurred. Love has its power, but so does order."

Another guardian, taller and with eyes like storm clouds, nodded. "James broke the rules, and the world bends under the weight of what you both have done. If we do nothing, the damage will spread—memories will unravel, days will repeat, stories will lose their endings."

Rachel shook her head, tears sliding down her cheeks. "We never wanted to hurt anyone. We just wanted to find each other. Was that so wrong?"

The third guardian, a quiet man with gentle hands, stepped closer and knelt to Rachel's level. "We know your pain. Many of us have loved and lost, too. But the laws of time are not cruel by

63

choice—they exist so that all stories, even the saddest ones, can be honored. To keep your love, you must accept the burden it brings. Or, we can heal the world and give you peace, but at the price of forgetting."

Rachel's grip on the pocket watch tightened. She looked at the guardians, at the swirling shadows and the books lining the walls, at the roses that still bloomed even as dawn neared. "I won't forget him. I accept the burden. I accept every memory, every cost. My story isn't just about loss—it's about love, too."

The woman guardian nodded, her expression softening. "Very well, Rachel. The pain will remain, but so will the joy. And the world will mend—slowly, carefully, around your memory and your courage."

As the guardians began to fade, the cold in the room eased. The air grew still, the shadows returned to their corners, and the light of morning crept back in. Rachel sank to the floor, tears falling freely, her heart aching with grief and gratitude all at once.

In that moment, Rachel understood that love could break rules and bring miracles, but it could also demand impossible choices. The guardians watched over her a moment longer, then disappeared, leaving Rachel alone with her memories—and with the quiet, stubborn hope that somewhere, James's story was not truly over.

As the golden morning spread across the bookstore, Rachel knelt on the floor, surrounded by scattered petals, the pocket watch cold in her hand. The guardians' words echoed in her mind: "To keep your love, you must accept the burden. Or, we can heal the world and give you peace, but at the price of forgetting."

The world outside seemed to hold its breath. Rachel stared at the watch, her memories of James rushing back in a flood—his eyes, his laughter, the letters, the impossible night of roses and magic. Every part of her ached with love and loss.

But the air in the bookstore shimmered with something fragile. Rachel felt the world trying to fix itself, the edges of her memories growing softer. She knew the guardians would soon return for her answer. If she chose to keep every memory, she might carry the pain forever—but if she let go, she would lose James for good.

Rachel stood, wiping the tears from her cheeks. She wandered between the bookshelves, trailing her hand over the spines. Each book held a memory, a moment she and James had shared—real or imagined. Was her love worth risking cracks in the world? Could she bear the weight of sorrow, knowing it was the price of something rare and true?

A gentle wind brushed through the shop, rustling a letter on the counter. Rachel picked it up, recognizing James's handwriting:

64

"If you must let me go to heal the world, do it bravely. But if you choose to remember, carry our story with pride. You made me real, Rachel. That is enough."

Rachel closed her eyes, letting his words settle in her heart. She thought of her mother, of all the times she had felt invisible and alone, of the courage it had taken to follow the clues and risk everything for love.

The guardians appeared once more, silent and waiting. The woman guardian asked softly, "What is your choice, Rachel Sullivan?"

Rachel straightened her shoulders, the pocket watch warm in her hand. She spoke clearly, even though her voice shook:

"I choose to remember. I choose to keep my love for James, no matter what it costs. I'd rather carry the pain of losing him than live in a world where our story never happened."

A hush fell across the shop. The guardians nodded, sadness and respect in their eyes.

"So be it," said the woman guardian. "Your memories will be your gift and your burden. The world will heal, and you will walk forward carrying every joy and every sorrow. Few are brave enough to choose the hard path, but love is never wasted."

As the guardians faded, light returned to the bookstore. The clocks ticked on, and Rachel stood alone, tears streaming down her face, but her heart was fierce and proud.

She would carry her story and James's memory through every pain and every sunrise, knowing she had chosen love, even when it was hardest.

Between worlds, where light and shadow melted into each other, James drifted—neither gone nor truly alive. He felt the pull of time unraveling behind him, the guardians' warnings echoing in the emptiness. But the memory of Rachel—her courage, her love—burned brighter than anything else.

He saw flashes of her alone in the bookstore, her face shining with tears and hope as she made her impossible choice. He heard her words: "I choose to remember. I choose to love." James's heart ached with longing. He had watched her carry the pain, bear the burden, refuse to let their story vanish.

James remembered the rules, the times he had watched tragedies unfold and done nothing, the many times he'd been forced to let go. But now, standing on the thin edge between stories, he realized love was not meant to only watch and wait. It was meant to change things—even if it meant breaking the world and risking himself once more.

He looked at the pocket watch in his hand, feeling its weight, its ticking heart. The silver was almost too bright to hold, pulsing with all the moments they had shared. The guardians' voices whispered in his mind: "Every change has a cost." But Rachel had taught him what faith looked like—what it meant to believe even when there was no proof.

James took a breath, deeper than any he'd taken before, and whispered into the shifting light, "Let me try, just once more. Let me give her what she gave me—a chance."

He pictured the rose blooming in winter, the lamplight in the shop, the sound of Rachel's laughter. He let his memories flow into the watch, filling it with every letter, every dream, every moment he and Rachel had found each other. As he turned the stem, time seemed to bend. Stories folded over each other—past and present swirling together.

The emptiness shuddered. A wave of warmth and gold swept through the space between worlds. James felt himself falling, not away from Rachel but toward her, guided by love instead of fear. He poured every last bit of hope and faith into the leap, willing the world to give them another chance.

For a heartbeat, everything was still. Then James saw the familiar glow of the bookstore, the rows of books, and the scent of roses and dust. Rachel stood there, tears shining in her eyes, the pocket watch pressed to her heart.

He reached for her. This time, his hand was solid, real. Their fingers touched, and the clocks in the shop chimed all at once, the sound filling every corner of the world.

Rachel gasped, her eyes wide with disbelief and joy. "James?"

He smiled, feeling her love wrap around him like light. "We took a leap of faith," he whispered, "and love rewrote our story."

In that moment, the rules bent, the guardians stepped aside, and time itself opened the door for two hearts brave enough to believe.

CHAPTER 11

The Blooming of the Timeless Rose

In the quiet of the bookstore, as Rachel and James stood reunited, a strange hush settled over the room. The air shimmered, and every clock on the walls stilled at the exact moment. Outside, the first light of dawn crept across the city, but inside, it felt as though time itself had paused to witness what would come next.

James reached out, gently wiping a tear from Rachel's cheek. The warmth of his hand felt real—more real than any dream or memory. Rachel leaned into his touch, hardly daring to believe this miracle had come true.

Suddenly, the air grew fragrant, sweet, and deep, like a memory of gardens in spring. Rachel and James turned toward the reading nook, where the rosebush from the night before had stood. Now, something remarkable was happening.

From the center of the bush, a single bud swelled and slowly unfurled. Its petals glowed with a soft, silvery light, edged in gold and blushing with a hint of pink. The bloom opened wider than any rose Rachel had ever seen, shining with dew that looked like tiny stars. It was a flower that belonged to no season, blooming in the heart of winter, defying every law of nature and time.

As the flower opened, the light around it grew brighter. For a moment, every book on the shelves seemed to glow; every memory, every sorrow, and every joy that had brought Rachel and James to this place sparkled in the golden air. The rose's scent filled the room, gentle and soothing, wrapping the two of them in comfort and hope.

James stepped forward and touched the petals, his fingers trembling with wonder. He turned to Rachel, his eyes shining. "This is for us," he said quietly. "Our love made it bloom. It's the proof that even when the world says something is impossible, love can make it real."

Rachel pressed her hand to her heart, tears slipping down her cheeks—not just of sadness, but of relief and joy. She realized that the flower was a promise, a symbol that what she and James shared could outlast even the rules of time.

67

As they knelt together beside the flower, the clocks in the shop began to tick once more. The golden light softened into the gentle glow of morning. Rachel knew that there would still be challenges, still be moments of pain and doubt, but now they had something rare and beautiful—something no guardian, no law, no distance could erase.

The mystical rose would always remind them: love could bloom in the strangest places, at the oddest times, and its petals would never fade.

Rachel and James looked at each other, hope shining between them. Their story was written not just in letters and memories, but in the rare, impossible bloom that glowed in the heart of the bookstore—a living promise that miracles could grow wherever love dared to take root.

The mystical rose continued to glow in the quiet bookstore, casting silver and gold light across the shelves and dust motes in the morning air. All around them, the clocks ticked out of rhythm—some racing ahead, some slowing down, others stopping for long, breathless moments. The line between one moment and the next seemed to blur, as if the world couldn't decide which story to tell.

Rachel stood close to James, her hands in his, their fingers intertwined as if they'd always belonged that way. The shop around them shimmered, sometimes clear and familiar, sometimes rippling with strange echoes of the past—books in languages Rachel couldn't read, shadows that looked like old friends, sunlight pouring through windows that were never really there.

For a heartbeat, Rachel caught a glimpse of herself as a girl, reading beneath the old oak tree. She saw James at her side in the park, laughing in a world where they'd always known each other. She saw all the roads she might have taken, all the years they'd both wandered, somehow leading them here.

James's eyes were full of wonder. He cupped Rachel's face gently, as if still afraid she might vanish. "I tried so hard to follow the rules," he whispered. "But love is stronger than time, stronger than fear. I would risk it all again just to hold you."

Rachel smiled through her tears. "I was lost for so long. But every story, every letter, every dream brought me here—to you. Maybe we were meant to find each other at the very edge of what's possible."

As the rose's glow spread, the shop seemed to dissolve into a place outside of time. For a few precious moments, there was no past or future—just the two of them, standing together in a world made by hope. The pocket watches in their hands beat in perfect unison, echoing the rhythm of their hearts.

The boundaries of time wavered all around them, sometimes pulling them forward, sometimes back. But in each reality, in every flickering image, Rachel and James found each other. They

68

were the constant in every version of their story—a thread of love weaving through every possibility.

Rachel wrapped her arms around James and held him close. "If the world changes, if time forgets us, promise you'll remember this moment."

James pressed his lips to her forehead, holding her tight. "I will. No matter what, I'll find you again. I'll write the story over and over until we have our happy ending."

As the clocks chimed together, the rose bloomed brighter, and the world settled at last. Rachel and James stood united, no longer divided by distance or time, their hearts steady and brave. Whatever tomorrow held—more magic, more struggle, or even the return of ordinary days—they faced it together.

And in the quiet after the miracle, Rachel knew that some stories were too strong for even time to break. She and James would always find their way back to each other, as long as hope endured.

As the morning sun climbed higher, the world inside the bookstore shimmered and pulsed with quiet magic. Rachel and James stood hand in hand, surrounded by the glowing rose, their pocket watches ticking in perfect rhythm. Then, as if the universe itself was holding its breath, time began to slow.

The sound of the clocks faded into a gentle hush. Dust motes hung in the air, frozen mid-drift. Rachel felt her heartbeat slow, her breaths growing long and deep, every second stretching into forever. She glanced at James and saw the same wonder in his eyes—a sense that anything was possible in this suspended moment.

Then the memories came.

It started as a soft wave—familiar and yet impossible. Rachel saw herself in places she'd never visited, wearing clothes from distant times. She saw a stone bridge in a rainy old city, where she and James, dressed in different faces, stood side by side, laughing beneath a single umbrella. She was a painter in a sunlit garden, and James was her muse, bringing her wildflowers every morning. In another life, she was a nurse in a crowded hospital, and James was a soldier, leaving her letters hidden in the spines of medical books.

Each memory came with a rush of feeling—love, loss, hope, and the constant ache of searching. She saw herself and James meeting and parting, again and again, across centuries and continents. Sometimes they were strangers who passed each other on quiet streets; sometimes they were family, friends, or secret lovers. In every story, their souls recognized each other, even if the world kept them apart.

James squeezed her hand, and his memories blended with hers. He saw Rachel as a scholar in a candlelit library, whispering poems in a language he barely remembered. He saw himself as a baker, leaving fresh bread at her window every morning before dawn. He recalled moments of joy—a dance under the stars, a promise made in a field of white flowers. And always, always, the sense of coming home when their eyes met.

The memories were overwhelming but beautiful. They flooded in—joys and heartbreaks, lives that had ended too soon, dreams left unfinished, but also second chances, and new beginnings. In the deepest part of her heart, Rachel knew these stories were real. She and James had been searching for each other through lifetimes, their souls always finding a way back.

As the magical glow faded and time slowly began to move again, Rachel and James leaned into each other, changed and comforted by the weight of all they had shared. They understood now that their love was bigger than one life, one story, or even one world.

Rachel smiled through her tears, the truth shining in her eyes. "We found each other, again and again."

James brushed his lips over her forehead. "And we always will. As long as there is time and hope, our story will never end."

As the last flickers of magic faded from the bookstore, the air settled into a quiet warmth. The mystical rose still glowed softly in the reading nook, a gentle reminder of the miracle they had just witnessed. Time began to move normally again—clock hands ticking, sunlight drifting through the windows, the world resuming its ordinary rhythm.

Rachel stood in James's arms, her cheek pressed to his shoulder, breathing in the quiet scent of books and roses. She could still feel echoes of the other lives they had lived, and it left her both full and hollow at the same time—a happiness so deep it almost hurt, and a sadness at knowing how many times they had lost and found each other.

James held her close, running his hand gently through her hair. "It's strange," he murmured. "We've had lifetimes together and apart, but this—right here, right now—feels the most real."

Rachel nodded, tears slipping down her cheeks. "I wish we could stay like this forever."

He smiled, soft and sad. "We both know how precious this is. Time isn't something we can trust—not after everything we've seen. But every moment with you feels like a gift. Even if it ends, I'll carry it with me, wherever or whenever I go."

Rachel closed her eyes, memorizing the feel of his arms around her, the sound of his heartbeat, the way his breath warmed her hair. She tried not to think about the ticking clocks or the shifting boundaries outside the shop. She just wanted to hold on to the peace, to the love, to the hope that had always pulled them back together.

70

They stood in silence, letting the weight of their story settle in their bones. Rachel's hands clung to James's shirt, unwilling to let go. "Promise me something?" she whispered. "Promise you'll never forget this — any of it. Even if we're pulled apart again."

James kissed her forehead, holding her tighter. "I promise. I'll remember every second, every laugh, every tear. I'll search for you in every life, in every world, until I find you again."

They swayed gently, surrounded by golden light and the hush of morning. Neither wanted to speak of goodbyes, but both knew that the world would eventually ask for its balance, that miracles like theirs always came at a cost.

But for now, time belonged to them.

Rachel pulled back just enough to look into James's eyes. "Whatever happens, thank you. For finding me, for loving me, for never giving up."

He brushed a tear from her cheek and smiled. "How could I? You are my story, Rachel. You always have been."

As the city woke outside, Rachel and James stayed in each other's arms, hearts joined in the fragile, perfect peace of knowing that even if time tried to tear them apart, love had given them this moment — and that was enough.

Outside the bookstore, the city stirred to life, as if nothing unusual had happened. But Rachel and James could feel it — a shift beneath their feet, a subtle trembling in the air. The mystical rose's bloom was not just a symbol of their love; it was a spark, a ripple sent through the fabric of time itself.

Rachel glanced at the clocks. Some ticked forward too quickly; others lagged behind, as if struggling to keep up with a new rhythm. She felt dizzy for a moment, her memories flickering in and out — some moments clear, others slipping away like water through her fingers.

James noticed it too. He looked out the bookstore window, squinting at the street outside. The bakery on the corner had a new sign, one he didn't remember. The statue in the park looked different — its base now carved with two names he recognized, names from a past life he thought he'd forgotten. A couple strolled by, holding hands, and for a second, Rachel saw herself and James reflected in their faces — two strangers given a second chance at love.

The phone in the shop rang, a sound that jolted Rachel from her daze. She picked it up and heard a familiar voice — Carla, her oldest friend. But the conversation felt strange, as if pieces were missing. Carla spoke of a book signing Rachel didn't remember, and a trip to the mountains they had never taken. When Rachel hung up, her hands shook.

"What's happening?" she whispered, her voice trembling.

71

James took her hands in his, steady and calm despite the fear in his eyes. "The rose changed something," he said softly. "It's not just us anymore. Time has shifted. Things are the same, but not the same."

All around them, small details kept slipping out of place. Customers entered the shop, smiling as if they'd always known Rachel and James as a couple. Old friends arrived with memories of parties and milestones neither of them remembered living. Even the letters James had written seemed to rewrite themselves, details changing in subtle, unnerving ways.

Rachel realized that the miracle she and James had shared was touching everyone they knew — echoing out into the world in ripples she could not control. For every happiness they gained, a memory vanished; for every new joy, a piece of the past faded away.

She squeezed James's hand, her heart pounding. "Did we do the right thing?" she asked, eyes shining with worry and hope.

James held her close. "We loved bravely, Rachel. Sometimes, changing history means losing parts of ourselves, but maybe it also means giving others a chance at happiness."

Outside, the city continued to shift and shimmer. The boundaries of reality, love, and memory blurred, but one thing remained sure—Rachel and James had changed the story, for better or worse.

As the day unfolded, neither knew what the future would bring. But as long as they faced it together, they were willing to pay the price, whatever the consequences, whatever the cost.

CHAPTER 12

The Twilight Encounter

———————— ✕ ————————

The morning sun filtered softly through the bookstore's windows, warm and golden. Rachel opened her eyes, curled up on the old green reading chair. The shop was quiet, dust swirling gently in the light. For a moment, she felt utterly alone, as if she'd just woken from a long, strange dream.

She sat up slowly, her heart heavy with questions. The memories of the night before were tangled in her mind—James's face, the miracle of the blooming rose, the dizzy swirl of clocks and time slipping sideways. But now, the world seemed ordinary again. There was no glow in the air, no shimmer on the shelves. The mystical rose was gone, replaced by a plain potted plant, its flowers closed tight.

Rachel pressed her hands to her eyes, trying to hold onto the fading magic. Had it all been a dream? A story her lonely heart had invented to fill the empty spaces of her life? She searched the shop for proof—something solid, something real.

On the counter, the silver pocket watch lay closed and still. She picked it up, holding it to her chest. The watch was warm, heavy, comforting. But as she turned it over in her hands, she saw nothing out of the ordinary. No initials, no secret inscription, just a simple old watch.

Rachel walked through the shop, calling James's name, her voice small and hopeful. There was no answer. She checked the reading nook, the clock tower illustration pinned on the wall, even the garden outside, but James was nowhere to be found.

Her phone buzzed. Carla's name appeared on the screen. Rachel hesitated, then answered. "Hey," she said softly.

Carla sounded bright and cheerful. "Morning! Just checking in. Are you still coming to lunch today?" There was no mention of James, no hint of the wild adventure that had filled Rachel's heart only hours before.

Rachel forced a smile. "Yes… I'll be there."

After she hung up, she sat on the window seat and watched people walking by outside. Had any of it really happened? Was James just a story she told herself—a longing so strong it felt like a memory?

Yet, as the sunlight warmed her face, Rachel noticed something strange. She still felt a quiet strength in her chest—a hope that hadn't been there before. And though the rosebush had vanished, a single white petal lay on the windowsill, soft and shining in the morning light.

Rachel pressed the pedal between the pages of her favorite book and closed her eyes. Whether James had been honest or only a dream, he had changed her. She carried his love like a secret, hidden in her heart, as proof that some stories—no matter how impossible—leave behind traces that can't be erased.

And as she whispered his name one last time, she found herself smiling, not with sadness, but with a quiet faith that somewhere, in some version of the world, love had found a way.

Rachel spent the morning in a quiet haze, carrying the weight of questions and memories as she worked around the shop. Every so often, she paused to look at the pocket watch, or to glance at the single white petal hidden in her book. With every hour, the world felt a bit more ordinary, but her heart wouldn't let go of the hope that something of James lingered.

As she straightened a shelf near the reading nook, Rachel spotted an envelope she hadn't noticed before. It was tucked between two thick novels, cream-colored and sealed with old-fashioned wax. Her breath caught in her throat. She recognized the elegant handwriting at once—James's looping script.

With trembling fingers, Rachel broke the seal and pulled out a single sheet of paper. The letter was short and bittersweet:

"My dearest Rachel,

If you are reading this, I am gone—but our story is not. Love leaves traces, even across worlds. Find the moments, follow the signs, and I will always be near. Yours, always—James."

Tears sprang to Rachel's eyes, but she smiled, feeling a warmth settle in her chest. She held the letter close, rereading it until the words became part of her.

She set the letter aside and noticed something peeking out from beneath the seat cushion of her favorite chair—a small, sepia-toned photograph. She lifted it gently. It showed the front of the bookstore many years ago, the door open, and sunlight pouring through. Standing just inside the doorway was a man in an old-fashioned coat, looking back at the camera with a gentle, hopeful smile. Rachel's breath hitched; the face was unmistakably James's, even if the details were blurred with age.

On the back, in faded pencil, were the words:

74

"Past Pages, waiting for you."

Rachel pressed the photograph to her heart, remembering all the times she had dreamed of him standing in that doorway. The picture made it real, somehow—a silent promise that he had truly been there, in some version of her life.

Last, as Rachel prepared to close the shop for the evening, she noticed a small box on the counter that hadn't been there before. Inside, nestled in velvet, was a delicate locket shaped like a rosebud. She opened it with careful fingers. Inside was a pressed white petal—just like the one on her windowsill—and a tiny scrap of parchment with the words:

"For all our stories, for all our tomorrows. Love, James."

Rachel's tears fell freely now, but she was no longer sad. The letter, the photograph, and the locket were proof that James had left her more than memories. He had left her faith in the impossible, courage to hope, and a gift she could hold close whenever she needed to remember she was loved.

Rachel fastened the locket around her neck, tucked the letter and photograph in her journal, and smiled at the soft glow in her heart. She knew she would never truly be alone, not as long as love could leave such beautiful signs behind.

It didn't take long for Rachel's friends to notice something different about her. The change was gentle, but steady—like the slow return of spring after a long, cold winter.

At lunch with Carla in a sunny café, Rachel listened closely and laughed more than usual. She no longer seemed lost in her thoughts, but present, her eyes shining with a quiet light. Carla watched her, a smile playing at the corners of her mouth.

"You seem happier, Rach," she said, reaching across the table to squeeze Rachel's hand. "I don't know what's gotten into you, but it looks good on you."

Rachel smiled, brushing a strand of hair behind her ear. "I think I just… realized that life is full of little miracles, if you're willing to see them. I spent so long being afraid of being alone, of missing out, of never finding what I needed. Now I know there's always hope. Even if things don't go the way we plan, something beautiful can still find us."

Carla raised an eyebrow, teasing. "Did you start reading self-help books, or did someone finally sweep you off your feet?"

Rachel only laughed, but her hand went unconsciously to the rosebud locket she wore around her neck. She didn't tell Carla the whole story—who would ever believe it?—but she felt no need to explain the magic that lingered in her heart.

At work, the change was even more apparent. Rachel was kinder to demanding customers, less anxious when things went wrong, and always quick with a gentle word or an encouraging smile. Her coworkers whispered about her newfound confidence and warmth. Some wondered if she'd fallen in love; others just felt drawn to the calm happiness she brought into every room.

Even in the bookstore, regular customers began to notice. Rachel rearranged the shelves so the sunlight poured onto the reading chairs. She planted fresh flowers by the door, and the whole place seemed lighter, friendlier, full of small wonders.

One afternoon, Dr. Westfield stopped by with a stack of old books. He paused at the counter, studying Rachel's face. "You've changed, my dear," he said softly. "There's a strength in you now — a hope I haven't seen in a long time."

Rachel nodded, gratitude swelling in her chest. "I just realized it's never too late for a new chapter, Dr. Westfield. Even the hardest stories can have moments of light."

As the days passed, Rachel carried her hope like a lantern through the ordinary world. She still missed James — some days the longing was sharp and sudden — but the pain was different now. It was laced with gratitude, courage, and the memory of a love that had taught her how to live bravely, even when she was afraid.

Rachel's friends could not see the magic, but they felt it in every smile, every gentle touch, and every word she spoke. Without even trying, Rachel became the proof that love and courage, once found, could light up not only her life but the lives of everyone around her.

A week after the strange night in the bookstore, Rachel's friends began to notice the difference in her. It was subtle at first, the way she smiled a little more easily and carried herself with a lighter step. The usual worry lines on her forehead had softened, and the distant, dreamy look in her eyes had been replaced with a calm certainty.

One afternoon, Carla dropped by Past Pages, her arms full of fresh flowers for the front window. She watched Rachel tidy the shelves, humming softly to herself. There was a glow about her — something peaceful and substantial.

"Rach," Carla said, setting the flowers down, "are you sure you're okay? You seem... I don't know, different lately. Happier, maybe?"

Rachel paused and turned, brushing a lock of hair behind her ear. "I am, Carla. For the first time in a long time, I think I finally believe things will work out. I just feel — braver, somehow. Like I can handle whatever comes next."

Carla gave her a searching look, then grinned. "That's good to hear. For a while, you seemed so lost in your head. Now you're... here, with us. With me."

Rachel blushed and smiled, her hand unconsciously touching the rosebud locket around her neck. She didn't try to explain. Some things could only be felt, not told.

At the bookstore, customers began to notice, too. Rachel greeted everyone with a genuine warmth, offering reading suggestions with newfound confidence and care. She took time to chat with children about their favorite stories, or to help an elderly man find a book he'd read as a boy. Even on busy days, she never seemed flustered—only content, as if she was exactly where she belonged.

One evening, as she locked up, Dr. Westfield stopped by to return a borrowed book. He studied her with a gentle curiosity. "You've changed, Rachel. There's a lightness about you now—a hope I haven't seen before."

Rachel looked out at the city, the streetlights flickering on. "I think I've learned not to be afraid of loving something, or someone, even if it hurts sometimes. There's always something to hope for, and always another chapter waiting to be written."

Her friends, her customers, even strangers passing through—everyone felt the shift. Rachel's fear had given way to faith, her old loneliness replaced by a quiet courage. It was as if she carried a secret lantern inside her, lighting the way for others just by being herself.

She still thought of James every day, but instead of aching, she found comfort in the memories and the little gifts he'd left behind. Rachel knew her story was not over, and whatever came next, she was ready to face it—not alone, but surrounded by the love and hope she'd found.

And as Carla hugged her goodbye that evening, she whispered, "Whatever it is, Rachel, I'm glad you found it. I've never seen you shine like this."

With each passing day, Rachel felt her life returning to its ordinary pace—morning sunlight in the bookstore windows, regulars stopping by for new stories, laughter over lunch with Carla, and warm, gentle evenings filled with the soft rustle of turning pages. But even as the routines of life returned, something deep and lasting had changed inside her.

She still wore the rosebud locket every day, sometimes touching it without thinking when the world felt too noisy or when a quiet longing swept through her. On some mornings, Rachel would find a single white petal on her pillow, even when the windows were closed and the garden was asleep. The petals never stayed for long—she tucked them away between the pages of her favorite books, quiet tokens that reminded her she was loved, even when no one was watching.

Sometimes, in the hush before opening the shop, Rachel would feel a presence—a warmth in the sunlight, a gentle breeze that carried the faintest scent of roses, or a flicker of movement in the reflection of a window. It was never enough to call a miracle, but consistently enough to fill her with hope.

There were days she missed James so much her heart ached. She would reread the letters he'd left, or trace the faded photograph of him at the shop door, and whisper his name into the quiet air. She wondered where he was now—if time had sent him to another story, another life, or if he was watching over her, just out of sight.

But even in those moments of missing him, Rachel felt comfort. She understood now that love was never really gone. It changed forms—it hid in old letters, in flowers, in memories, in the quiet strength that carried her through the day. Love was in the way she smiled at strangers, the stories she shared, and the courage she found to open her heart again.

Rachel's friends noticed how she radiated a soft joy, a steady faith that things would be all right. They did not know the actual reason behind her glow, but they trusted her kindness and let themselves believe in the possibility of magic.

One evening, as she locked the shop and stepped outside, Rachel looked up at the sky. The stars were beginning to appear, bright and patient, shining over the city just as they always had. She took a slow, steady breath and smiled.

"I love you, wherever you are," she whispered, feeling the truth of it ripple through her, across time, across distance. She knew he heard her, somehow.

Rachel walked home through the quiet streets, knowing that their story—her story—was far from over. She felt a peace she had never known before. Love endures, she realized, not just in miracles or memories, but in every small act of hope and kindness.

And in the deep, unseen places of the world, Rachel knew, love waited—growing, glowing, ready for the next chapter, no matter how long it took to find its way home.

CHAPTER 13

The Guardian's Warning

One night, long after the city had fallen asleep and the rain tapped gently at her window, Rachel drifted off in her reading chair. She had been reading an old novel by lamplight, the rosebud locket warm against her skin, when her eyelids grew heavy and she slipped into a dream.

In the dream, the bookstore was filled with soft, golden mist. The clocks on the walls ticked in slow, gentle waves, and the air was sweet with the scent of blooming roses. Rachel stood alone, the silence so deep she could hear her own heartbeat.

From the shadows by the door, a figure emerged—tall, dressed in a long black coat, their hair streaked with silver. Their eyes shone with the wisdom and sadness of countless ages. Rachel knew at once: this was one of the guardians, a time-keeper, come to visit her at last.

The guardian smiled kindly, as if they had known Rachel for a very long time. "Do not be afraid," they said, their voice like wind through leaves. "You have walked a difficult path with courage and heart. The world has changed because of your story."

Rachel felt no fear, only curiosity. "Why are you here?"

The guardian stepped closer, glancing at the locket around her neck. "I came to tell you what so few ever learn: Love and memory are never wasted. You chose bravely, Rachel. Your pain, your hope, your longing—they shaped time itself. And though you paid a price, you have given others the courage to believe in what cannot be seen."

Rachel's eyes filled with tears. "Will I ever see James again? Is there hope for another chapter?"

The guardian reached out, brushing a gentle hand against Rachel's hair. "All stories continue, even when the pages seem to end. The boundaries between worlds are thinner than you know. When you love without fear, when you remember with kindness, you open doors for miracles—large and small. James's love endures, and so does yours. In dreams, in signs, in the quiet moments between waking and sleep, you will find each other again."

Rachel closed her eyes, comforted by the truth in the guardian's words. The golden mist swirled around her, and the clocks began to chime, their music soft and sweet.

Before leaving, the guardian placed a small white rose in Rachel's hand—a final gift, impossibly perfect, its petals shimmering with dew. "Keep this close," the guardian whispered. "Whenever you doubt, let it remind you: Love, once given, is never lost."

Rachel woke with the sunrise, the golden light spilling across the shop floor. On her lap, where her dream hand had clutched the rose, lay a single white petal, shining with dew that had not come from any rain.

She pressed the petal to her heart and smiled. Whatever the future held, she knew she would keep loving, keep hoping, and keep believing. And somewhere, she trusted, time would bend once more—and her story with James would begin again.

Rachel lingered in the golden dream, the white rose trembling in her hand. The guardian stood before her, their eyes deep and knowing, the air around them rippling with quiet power.

"Rachel," the guardian said softly, "you have traveled further into the heart of time and memory than most ever dare. But every gift has a shadow. Every miracle brings with it a warning."

Rachel listened, her heart beating fast. She remembered the world shifting, memories changing, the bittersweet price she and James had paid to find each other. "What must I do?" she asked, her voice small but steady.

The guardian's expression grew serious, a sadness flickering across their face. "Tampering with time is never simple, and never safe. Each change sends ripples—moments lost, people altered, stories rewritten. You have felt this already: friends who remember things you do not, places that look familiar and strange at once, memories that slip and slide like water."

Rachel nodded, thinking of Carla's stories that didn't quite fit, of photographs and books that seemed to rearrange themselves overnight. She felt both grateful for what she had gained and anxious for what might yet be lost.

"Hold tight to the truth of your own heart," the guardian continued, their voice gentle but firm. "It is easy to be tempted—to wish for one more day, one more miracle, one more chance to undo pain or fix a regret. But even love can become a chain if it tries to bend the world too far."

Rachel's fingers closed around the rose, the dream world flickering as if caught between past and future. "Is it wrong to want another miracle? To hope I'll see James again?"

The guardian shook their head. "Hope is never wrong. But the world asks us to carry our stories with courage, not to erase the parts that hurt. Time has given you a gift—a memory

80

strong enough to last, and a heart brave enough to love. If you seek to change more, you may lose yourself and the ones you love."

Rachel felt a shiver of fear but also a sense of resolve. She realized that the most incredible courage was not in rewriting the past, but in living fully in the present—with gratitude, forgiveness, and faith that the future would offer new chapters.

The guardian placed a hand on her shoulder. "Let your memories guide you, not rule you. When you are ready for another miracle, it will come not by force, but by the quiet strength of hope and kindness. Trust your story, Rachel. And let love shape what comes next."

The golden light brightened, and the clocks in the dream all chimed at once. Rachel woke with a start, her hand still clutching the white rose. The shop was silent, the morning fresh. She understood now: the danger was not in remembering, but in letting the past control her life.

Rachel smiled and placed the rose by the register. She would live her story bravely, grateful for every pain and miracle. And in her heart, she kept the guardian's warning close, ready for whatever time and memory would bring.

Days passed, but the ache in Rachel's heart did not fade. She found herself reaching for the locket at her throat, rereading James's letters and tracing his photograph with trembling fingers. The memory of their love burned bright, but so did the warning the guardian had given her. Still, Rachel could not help wondering—was it truly wrong to try to find James again? Was a second miracle too much to hope for?

One evening, rain drummed softly on the bookstore windows as Rachel tidied the shelves alone. She paused at the counter, staring at the white rose the guardian had left. She remembered the way time had bent, the worlds that had blurred, the taste of hope and magic in the air. If she just reached out—if she dared to bend the rules one more time—maybe she could bring James back to her.

The thought haunted her through sleepless nights. In her dreams, she saw James on the other side of a glass wall, reaching for her with longing in his eyes. Sometimes she woke with her hand pressed against her own reflection, the emptiness of her arms almost too much to bear.

One night, unable to sleep, Rachel unlocked the old desk drawer and spread out every clue she had left: the pocket watch, the pressed petals, the letters, the photograph, the locket. She whispered James's name into the quiet, begging for a sign. If there was even the slightest chance—one more riddle to solve, one last message to find—she wanted it, needed it.

The temptation grew stronger when she discovered a hidden compartment in the back of the pocket watch, something she had never noticed before. Inside was a tiny, folded scrap of parchment. On it was a single line in James's hand:

"If you seek me, follow the hour the rose first bloomed."

81

Rachel's heart leapt. She knew the moment the clock had struck twelve, the night the miracle occurred. What if she returned to the bookstore at that hour, with all of James's gifts in hand? What if she retraced every step, whispered every word, pleaded with time and fate, and every guardian she could not see?

The possibilities pulled at her with almost unbearable force. She could risk everything—her memories, her world, her very self—to find him. The warning echoed: each change carries a cost. Would she lose friends, change her past, or even lose the memory of James altogether?

Rachel stood in the empty shop at midnight, trembling with hope and fear. She stared at the glowing face of the mystical rose, her hand hovering over the watch.

"Please," she whispered into the silence. "One more chance. Just one."

But as the hour passed, and no miracle came, Rachel felt the weight of the choice before her. The most significant test of love, she realized, was not always in fighting fate, but sometimes, in letting go. Tears filled her eyes, but her heart grew steadier. She would not force a miracle at any cost. She would trust her story and trust James's love, wherever it found her next.

Rachel stood in the center of the quiet bookstore, the mystical rose glowing softly in the corner, the pocket watch cold in her hand. The city outside was silent, the night pressing close to the windows. The moment felt heavy, like the world itself was waiting for her to decide.

Her heart ached with longing. She could still feel James's presence in the room: in the way the lamplight bent across the shelves, in the scent of roses in the air, in the ticking of clocks that seemed to echo with his laughter. Every part of her wanted to reach for him, tried to call him back, to risk everything for one more moment together.

But the guardian's warning hung in her mind like a bell: Every change carries a cost. The more she tried to bend time, the more the world would slip and unravel. Rachel had seen it already — memories rewriting themselves, friends losing pieces of the past, her own story growing full of gaps and shadows. She remembered the confusion in Carla's eyes, the strange new photographs, the way certain moments no longer fit together.

Rachel paced the shop, the two sides of her heart at war. Was it selfish to want James back, to chase another miracle, even if it meant risking the lives and memories of everyone she loved? Or was it wrong to give up, to settle for loneliness and regret when she knew in her bones that love was worth any price?

She pressed the watch to her chest, feeling the cold metal steady her pulse. She thought of James's last letter: *"You made me real. Carry our story with pride."* He had given her hope, not just in love, but in herself. He had trusted her to know the difference between what could be changed and what must be protected.

82

Rachel walked to the window and looked out at the sleeping city. The stars above seemed impossibly far away, but she drew strength from their patience. She imagined all the stories unfolding in the world—lives overlapping, memories building and breaking, each one precious and fragile.

Tears filled her eyes, but she did not wipe them away. "I love you, James," she whispered into the darkness. "But I can't break the world for us—not if it means losing what's good and true for everyone else."

In that quiet moment, Rachel chose duty. She would protect time, honor the sacrifices she and James had made, and trust that their love would find its own way—unforced, unbroken, and as accurate as any miracle.

She sat down, letting the peace of her decision fill her. The longing in her heart would never fade, but it would become something new: the courage to live fully, the hope that love—if strong enough—could survive anything, even the boundaries of time.

And as she drifted to sleep, Rachel felt the soft brush of a dream, a promise that love, when given freely and bravely, could never truly be lost.

Rachel stood in the soft lamplight of the bookstore, the magical rose shedding a gentle glow across the shelves. In her hands, she held the silver pocket watch and the rosebud locket, both heavy with memories and longing. Her heart still ached for James, but the storm inside her had quieted. She knew what she had to do.

She strolled to the center of the shop, looking around at the rows of books, the favorite chair where James had left his photograph, the spot on the counter where she had first found his letter. These were the places that held their story—proof that their love had shaped her life, even if the world itself was fragile.

Rachel drew a deep breath, feeling the weight and warmth of her memories. "I love you, James," she said softly, speaking into the quiet room. "I will always love you. But I can't bend time anymore. I can't risk the lives, stories, and hopes of everyone else just for one more miracle. I want to honor you, not break the world."

She thought of her friends, her customers, the way the city itself seemed to tremble when time shifted. She remembered the guardians' warning and the strange moments when her memories slipped away, replaced by shadows and missing days. Rachel understood now: love was strongest when it was gentle, when it gave as much as it asked.

She knelt before the mystical rose and placed the watch and locket at its base. "This is my promise," she whispered, her voice steady with new resolve. "I will carry your love with me, always. I will let it make me kinder, braver, and more hopeful. But I will protect this world, too. I won't let longing or pain push me to risk everything again."

83

For a moment, the rose glowed brighter, as if it heard her words and blessed her vow. Rachel felt a sense of peace and release—a sense that she had finally chosen the right path.

Standing, she brushed a tear from her cheek and smiled. Her grief would not disappear, but neither would her gratitude. She could love James without breaking the rules of time. She could hold his memory close and still move forward, living her life as fully as she could.

Rachel walked to the front window and watched the city waking up—the first rays of sun lighting the rooftops, people starting their day. She realized her story wasn't ending. It was only changing shape. She would write new chapters, find new joys, and share the hope that love— true, gentle, and brave—could last, even without miracles.

In her heart, Rachel repeated her vow, feeling stronger and lighter than she had in years:

I will honor our love and protect the world we both cherish. I will remember, and I will live.

And as the new day began, Rachel knew she was exactly where she was meant to be—at the start of something beautiful, carrying her love into every tomorrow.

CHAPTER 14

A Rift in Time

For a few days after making her vow, Rachel felt lighter, more at peace, more certain of her path. But as the week wore on, subtle cracks began to show in the world around her, small at first, then growing harder to ignore.

It started with déjà vu. Rachel would be shelving books in the shop and suddenly feel she had done it before—not just yesterday, but again and again, as if caught in a loop. She'd greet a customer and know, before they spoke, exactly what book they would ask for. Once, she found herself answering the phone, only to realize she had already had the same conversation with Carla earlier that morning.

At first, Rachel dismissed it as stress or lack of sleep. But then, the strangeness deepened. One afternoon, Carla stopped by the shop, a puzzled look on her face. "Rach, do you remember the trip we took to the mountains last fall?" Carla asked, brow furrowed. "I keep finding pictures from it, but I can't remember actually going. Was it real?"

Rachel's heart skipped. She remembered planning the trip, even packing her bag, but the actual journey was a blur—a collection of snapshots and stories, but no living memory.

As the days went on, more odd things happened. The clock on the bookstore wall began ticking backward for a few seconds at a time. Customers mentioned books that didn't exist, or swore they'd read something in her shop that Rachel had never stocked. She found an old letter from James tucked in a book she didn't remember reading, with a date that didn't match any year she had ever lived.

Strangest of all were the moments when Rachel would pause and feel like the world had slipped, as if a film was skipping frames. She'd blink and find herself standing in a different room, her hands holding a book she hadn't picked up. Once, she caught her own reflection in the shop's window and didn't recognize the expression on her face—hopeful and lost all at once.

The people around her were affected, too. Dr. Westfield came into the shop, searching for a book he had given Rachel just last week. When she handed it to him, he frowned. "Didn't I already read this?" he wondered aloud. "Or was that someone else?" Friends forgot birthdays, mixed up names, and sometimes looked at Rachel as if seeing her for the first time.

Rachel's heart grew heavy with worry. She understood that time was unraveling, that her choices and her longing for James had rippled out further than she ever meant. The world was full of memories that didn't belong and stories that didn't quite fit.

Standing alone in the shop at dusk, Rachel placed her hand over her heart and whispered, "I'm sorry." She knew now — her story and James's were woven tightly into the world's tapestry, and even the gentlest wishes could tug at the threads holding everything together.

Outside, the city glimmered with ordinary life, but Rachel saw the edges fraying. She wondered: Was there still time to set things right?

The strange events grew worse with each passing day. The clocks in the bookstore ticked in odd rhythms, sometimes skipping minutes, pausing as if unsure whether to move forward or back. Friends grew confused, memories slipped away, and Rachel's heart felt pulled in two by guilt and longing.

One evening, as dusk settled over the city, Rachel sat at her desk surrounded by letters, petals, and photographs. She pressed the locket to her chest, eyes closed, whispering James's name into the growing quiet.

Then, as if called across the worlds by her longing, James appeared. It was not like a dream — he was there, standing in the lamplight, real and uncertain, his face shadowed with worry.

"Rachel," he said, his voice a mix of relief and fear. "I felt it too. The unraveling — the way memories blur and the world loses its shape. I think we broke more than we meant to."

Rachel rose, crossing the room to take his hands. His touch was warm, as solid as it had ever been, and it filled her with bittersweet hope. "We have to fix this, James. If we do nothing, the world might fall apart. I can't let that happen — even if it means losing you again."

James nodded, his eyes shining with love and regret. "I don't want to lose you either. But we have to find a way to mend the story — to set time right, even if it costs us our happy ending."

Together, they searched the letters and clues they had gathered. Rachel read old notes aloud, tracing codes and dates, searching for patterns. James examined the pocket watch, listening for the moments when its ticking matched the strange pulses of the city outside.

They remembered the night of the mystical rose — the hour the clocks all stopped and their love rewrote a piece of history. "Maybe we can return to that moment," James said quietly. "Maybe if we go back, we can make a different choice. We can leave the world untouched, even if it means saying goodbye."

Rachel's voice trembled, but she nodded. "We owe it to everyone we love, to everyone whose memories are slipping away. We had our miracle, James. Maybe it's time to give the world back its balance."

They planned carefully, laying out the pocket watches, petals, and letters on the table. As midnight approached, the clocks all chimed together, the city outside holding its breath. Rachel and James stood side by side, hearts joined in courage.

"If this is goodbye," Rachel whispered, "I want you to know I would choose you in every life. But I want the world to keep turning, and I want you to be safe, even if I have to let you go."

James pressed his forehead to hers. "I love you, Rachel. No ending can ever take that away."

As the final chime echoed, they joined hands, ready to face whatever sacrifice was needed to heal the world—even if it meant their story would become only a memory.

As Rachel and James stood together in the lamplight, preparing to face the final moment, an uneasy silence settled between them. They could feel the weight of their choices in the heavy air—the frayed edges of time, the memories slipping away, the world trembling just out of sight.

Suddenly, the guardian appeared at the edge of the bookstore, half-shadow and half-light. Their eyes were full of sorrow and wisdom, and the golden mist that followed them carried the scent of roses and endings.

"You must know the truth before you choose," the guardian said gently, their voice echoing in the quiet. "Love is a miracle, but every miracle comes at a price."

Rachel's heart beat painfully. She looked at James, seeing the hope and fear in his eyes. "What is the cost?" she whispered.

The guardian moved through the shop, their fingers brushing over the spines of books, pausing at the letters and pocket watches. "Your story, beautiful as it is, has tangled the threads of many lives. For every memory you've rewritten, another has faded. For every moment you've changed, another has slipped away."

They gestured toward the window, and for a brief, dizzy moment, Rachel saw glimpses of her friends and customers—Carla searching through her purse for a lost key she never owned, Dr. Westfield looking at Rachel with confusion, unable to recall why he visited the shop. Across the city, strangers forgot birthdays, lovers lost the feeling that first brought them together, and children remembered parents' faces but not their names.

Tears welled in Rachel's eyes. "We never meant for anyone to be hurt. We just wanted to hold on to each other."

The guardian nodded, their expression gentle but firm. "That is the nature of miracles that bend time. They ripple outward, touching every story—sometimes in small ways, sometimes in ways that can never be undone."

James's voice was thick with sorrow. "If we let go—if we undo what we've changed—will the world be whole again?"

"There is always a price for healing," the guardian said. "Your love has been a gift to you both, but it cannot exist at the cost of so many others' happiness and truth. If you choose to set things right, you may lose your memories, your story together, perhaps even the chance to meet again in this life. But others will find their missing moments, their lost loved ones, and the world will heal."

Rachel felt her heart breaking. She saw in James's face the same pain, the same longing to choose what was right. She squeezed his hand, drawing courage from the depth of their love.

"We have to let go," she whispered, her voice trembling. "Not just for us, but for everyone whose lives we've touched. If our story must become a memory, let it be a gift, not a burden."

James nodded, tears shining in his eyes. "I would choose you in every lifetime, Rachel. But now, I choose what is good for all."

As they prepared for goodbye, Rachel knew that true love sometimes meant sacrifice—and that the most incredible stories were the ones that let the world keep spinning, even when hearts ached for more.

The bookstore was filled with stillness, the mystical rose glowing faintly in the corner. The guardian's words echoed through Rachel's heart as she held James's hand. They stood at the crossroads, the choice clear but almost too painful to bear.

Rachel gazed into James's eyes, searching for the answer she hoped she wouldn't have to find. The shop around them flickered—images blurring, books rearranging themselves, the clocks ticking out of sync. In her mind, she saw the faces of friends and strangers, lives slipping away at the edges, entire memories dissolving like fog at dawn.

"If we stay together," James whispered, his voice thick with love and sorrow, "the world might never heal. The people we care about... even people we'll never know... their stories will keep unraveling. There will be chaos. Lost time, lost lives."

Rachel's hand trembled in his. "But if we let go, we lose everything. Our memories, our story, all the magic that brought us here."

James pressed his forehead to hers, and for a moment, nothing else existed—just the two of them, holding on as the universe trembled around them. "Love doesn't always mean holding on, Rachel. Sometimes it means letting go, so something bigger can be saved. We had our miracle, but maybe it's time to give the world back its balance."

A single tear rolled down Rachel's cheek. She looked at the locket and the pocket watch—symbols of a love that had already bent reality—and then at the faces in her memories: Carla's laughter, Dr. Westfield's kindness, the countless customers and friends who made up the world she called home.

The guardian stepped closer, their presence calm but urgent. "You must decide now. Remain together, and chaos will grow—lives will continue to unravel. Or part, and the world will heal. The cost is great, but the choice is yours alone."

Rachel's heart pounded. She wanted to fight fate, to hold onto James and defy the world one more time. But she saw the cost in the trembling of the shop, the shadows at the edge of every memory. She understood now: real love was brave enough to let go.

"I don't want to forget you," she whispered, tears shining in her eyes. "But I want the world to be whole. I want people to have their stories back, even if it means losing ours."

James cupped her face in his hands, his touch gentle and full of promise. "We'll find each other again, Rachel. In another life, another world. Our love will endure, even if we must part now."

Rachel nodded, her voice small but strong. "Then let's do what's right. Let's give the world a chance to heal."

Hand in hand, hearts breaking but full of courage, Rachel and James made their choice. The mystical rose glowed bright, then faded. The clocks in the shop stilled. The guardian offered a final, grateful nod.

As their love story began to dissolve into memory, Rachel closed her eyes, trusting that true love could never be erased—even if the world needed them to let go.

The air in the bookstore shimmered with a soft, golden light, as if the world wanted to make their goodbye beautiful. Rachel and James stood close, holding each other for the last time, surrounded by the quiet magic of their story.

Rachel felt the weight of the moment—the way everything seemed to pause, the hush before something precious is lost. She pressed her face to James's chest, listening to the steady beat of his heart, hoping she would never forget the sound.

James wrapped his arms around her and breathed in the scent of her hair, the feeling of her warmth. He wanted to hold onto every detail—her laughter, her tears, the strength in her eyes—so he could carry them into whatever future waited for him.

Rachel looked up at him, her cheeks wet with tears, but her voice clear and full of promise. "No matter what happens, I'll always love you. If I forget, if time takes everything from me, I want you to know — I'll be looking for you in every story, every sunrise, every dream."

James smiled, his eyes shining. "I'll find you again, Rachel. I'll write you letters in the stars if I have to. I'll search every life until we find our way back. Nothing — not even time — can keep me from you."

The bookstore around them began to blur, as if the world was gently closing the chapter. The mystical rose faded, its petals turning to light. The clocks stopped ticking, and the shop was filled with the sound of their quiet breaths.

Rachel pressed the rosebud locket into James's hand. "Keep this, wherever you go. Let it remind you of our love, even if you can't remember my name."

James closed his hand around the locket, tucking it close to his heart. "I'll carry it always. And if you ever find it again, you'll know it's me."

For a moment, time stretched thin and still. Rachel and James gazed at each other, hearts overflowing with love and sorrow and hope.

"I'll look for you in the next lifetime," Rachel whispered, her voice trembling but full of faith.

"And I'll wait for you," James replied, "however long it takes."

They leaned in, sharing one last, gentle kiss — a promise sealed across lifetimes, a vow that nothing could break.

As the golden light faded, Rachel felt James slipping away, his touch growing lighter, his image softer. She clung to his memory, determined to hold onto the feeling, the hope, the certainty that this was not an ending, but a beginning.

And when the magic finally faded, leaving only sunlight and silence in the shop, Rachel knew, deep in her soul, that their love would find its way back — no matter how many stories it took, no matter how much time tried to keep them apart.

CHAPTER 15

Eternal Echoes

The golden glow faded, leaving the bookstore in soft, familiar morning light. Rachel stood in the hush, her arms wrapped around herself, her heart both empty and full. For a long time, she did not move. She simply listened to the silence, to the faint ticking of the clocks, to the memories drifting through her mind.

The shop looked the same as it always had—shelves full of books, sunlight spilling across the rug, the gentle creak of wood as the building settled into a new day. But Rachel knew everything had changed. She felt it in the quiet ache of her chest and the calm that had taken root inside her.

She strolled through the aisles, her fingers trailing over the books she and James had once touched together. The magical rose was gone now, its petals only a memory, but she imagined she could still smell its sweetness in the air. The locket was no longer in her hand, but the warmth of James's final embrace lingered, an invisible comfort she could carry forward.

Rachel stopped at the window seat and looked out at the city. The world outside moved on as always—people hurrying down the street, children laughing, shopkeepers opening their doors. She wondered how many of them had ever known how close they'd come to losing their stories, how a single love could change everything and still leave so much of life untouched.

She thought of all she had seen: the letters, the treasure hunt, the miracles and the warnings, the temptation to change the world for love. She remembered the guardians and the gentle sorrow in their eyes, the promises she and James had made to protect the balance of things, even at the cost of their own happiness.

Rachel sat down in her favorite chair, the one by the window where she and James had shared their dreams. She pressed a hand to her heart, feeling both loss and peace. She had wanted a miracle, but found something better—a story of courage, sacrifice, and the kind of love that survives even the end of magic.

She closed her eyes and let the memories settle, soft and golden, neither clinging nor fading. "Thank you," she whispered, not to anyone in particular but to the story itself, for giving her

91

hope, for teaching her to love bravely, for letting her believe that the impossible was worth fighting for.

As the city bustled outside and sunlight warmed her face, Rachel realized her journey was not over. She would keep living, keep hoping, keep honoring the love she had found. One chapter had ended, but the story of her life would go on—written in every act of kindness, every page she turned, every time she let her heart open to wonder.

Rachel smiled, gentle and true. She was alone now, but she was not lonely. Her story would always be full of loss, of hope, and of a love that even time could not erase.

In the weeks that followed, Rachel moved through life with a new sense of strength. The sadness of losing James remained, but it was gentle now—a steady ache that reminded her of what she had survived, and all she had gained. Her days in the bookstore felt brighter. She faced each morning with calm courage, knowing she could handle whatever came, because she had already faced the impossible and chosen what was right.

Rachel noticed the change in herself most in small moments. When a customer grew impatient, she met them with patience and understanding. When her friend Carla was upset about a lost memory, Rachel listened quietly and comforted her, not with answers, but with a warm embrace and a smile. She no longer hid from her loneliness or doubted her worth. Instead, she welcomed every feeling—joy and pain, love and loss—as a part of her own unfolding story.

She felt wiser, too. She understood now that some things could never be controlled, no matter how hard she tried. Time would keep moving, stories would change, and people would come and go. But the love she and James had shared—that could never be erased. It lived in her kindness to strangers, her courage in challenging moments, and her hope for whatever the future would bring.

Rachel carried her memories with grace, letting them guide her instead of holding her back. When she looked at the shelves in the bookstore, she didn't see only the past, but a thousand possibilities for the future. Every new customer, every new book, every smile was a reminder that her story was still being written.

One evening, Rachel closed the shop and sat by the window, watching the city glow with the colors of sunset. She pressed her hand over her heart and whispered, "Thank you, James." She meant it—not just for the love they'd shared, but for everything their story had taught her.

She realized she was no longer afraid of losing or starting over. She had learned that true love was not about holding on forever, but about becoming the best version of herself, even after goodbye. She could live bravely, laugh easily, and face the unknown with trust.

Her friends noticed the difference, and strangers found themselves drawn to her gentle wisdom. The world around her seemed softer and kinder, as if Rachel's newfound strength had quietly changed it, too.

As the stars appeared and the city fell silent, Rachel felt at peace. She was grateful for every chapter—good and bad—that had brought her to this moment. And she knew, deep in her soul, that the story of her love for James would live on, giving her courage and wisdom for all the days still to come.

She was not only the keeper of a great love, but the author of a new, stronger life.

As the seasons turned, Rachel found comfort in the routines of her days. Yet, she often sensed that she was not truly alone. Slight, gentle hints of James's spirit lingered at the edges of her life, soft as the touch of a breeze or the memory of a dream.

Sometimes, when she needed courage, Rachel would find a white petal on her windowsill, fresh as morning dew. No matter how tightly the windows were shut, the petal always appeared— resting on her notebook, tucked inside a book she was about to read, or pressed beneath the cup she lifted for her tea. Each time she smiled, a wave of gratitude washed over her heart.

On her hardest days, when doubt threatened to return, Rachel would hear a favorite song playing faintly on the shop radio—a song she'd once danced to with James, though she never remembered adding it to any playlist. The music gave her hope, lifting her spirits and reminding her that love could still find her, even through something as simple as a melody.

In the bookstore, Rachel sometimes found books out of place—old volumes she and James had read together, mysteriously appearing at the top of a stack or set aside on the counter, waiting to be discovered. Once, while cleaning behind the counter, she found a scrap of parchment tucked inside a novel. In James's familiar handwriting, it read: *"Believe in new beginnings."*

Whenever the rosebush in her window bloomed out of season—a single white flower glowing in the winter sun—Rachel knew James was close, sending her strength to face the world, no matter what.

Her dreams, too, were sometimes filled with his presence. She would walk through a city made of golden light and see him waiting on a bridge, smiling, always just ahead. She would wake with her heart calm, sure that his promise—to find her in every lifetime—remained true.

Rachel shared these gentle signs with no one, keeping them as secret treasures. She didn't need anyone to believe her; it was enough to know that love did not vanish, but changed form, weaving quietly through her life. James's guidance was never loud or obvious, but always there when she needed it most—a steady whisper in the silence, a warm touch when she felt lost.

93

As spring returned, Rachel placed a fresh rose by the shop window, remembering their journey and the vows they had made. She greeted every customer with warmth, shared stories with friends, and trusted her heart to lead her forward.

She knew now that the greatest loves don't disappear when life moves on. They become part of the world itself—showing up in music, in flowers, in laughter, and in new hopes. James was with her still, in all the small ways that mattered, helping her write each new page of her life.

And with every sign, Rachel felt a little braver, a little lighter, confident that love's magic would always remain.

The bell above the bookstore door chimed softly as Rachel unlocked the shop early one morning. Today was special—a day she had dreamed about for a long time. After all she had been through, after all the love and loss, she was ready to share a new part of her story with the world.

In a quiet corner of *Past Pages*, Rachel had created a new space, a place filled with light and wonder. She called it **"Letters Across Time."** Shelves lined with beautifully bound journals, vintage stationery, and old-fashioned writing tools filled the nook. Each shelf held letters— some real, some fictional, some inspired by stories of love, hope, and connection across distances and decades.

Rachel arranged a small display near the entrance, featuring a delicate rosebud locket and a silver pocket watch—tokens from her own journey with James. A framed letter, written in graceful script, shared a glimpse of their story:

"Sometimes love crosses time and space in the smallest of letters—whispers from one heart to another, carrying hope and dreams across the years."

She smiled as she thought about how far she had come—from feeling lost and alone to creating a place where others could find their own stories of courage and connection. The *Letters Across Time* section was her gift to the world, a reminder that every story mattered and every love was worth cherishing.

Throughout the day, customers wandered into the nook, drawn by the soft glow of the reading lamps and the gentle scent of old paper and roses. Children wrote notes to faraway grandparents, teenagers left secret messages for first loves, and elderly visitors found comfort in letters that reminded them of their own youth and hopes.

Rachel helped a young woman choose a journal, sharing a knowing smile. "Sometimes, writing down your story is the first step to finding yourself again," she said gently.

Later, a man in his seventies approached, holding a worn envelope. "I've carried this letter for decades," he said quietly. "I think it's time to share it."

94

Rachel nodded, touched by the trust and the quiet bravery in his eyes. She helped him find a place to display the letter, part of a growing collection that celebrated love's enduring power.

As the sun set and the shop grew quiet, Rachel sat in the nook, feeling a deep peace. She touched the rosebud locket around her neck and looked at the letters glowing softly on the shelves. Her journey with James had changed her, but it had also given her a purpose — to be a keeper of stories, a guardian of hope.

In *Past Pages*, in the heart of the city, *Letters Across Time* was a sanctuary — a place where love, memory, and courage lived on, carried gently in ink and paper, waiting to connect hearts across all the years to come.

The bookstore was quiet, bathed in the soft glow of afternoon light filtering through the windows. Rachel sat behind the counter in the **Letters Across Time** nook, her fingers tracing the worn edges of a journal filled with messages of love, hope, and courage. The gentle hum of pages turning and whispered stories filled the air like a comforting song.

As she looked up, the bell above the door tinkled softly. A young woman stepped inside, her eyes wide with wonder as she took in the cozy nook filled with letters and memories. Rachel smiled warmly, welcoming her with a nod.

While greeting the visitor, Rachel noticed something resting on the edge of the counter — a plain, cream-colored envelope, unlike any she had seen before. It had no stamp, no return address. Her heart skipped as she picked it up, recognizing the delicate, flowing handwriting instantly.

Her fingers trembled as she broke the seal and unfolded the letter inside.

"Dear Rachel," it began, *"If you are reading this, it means you have opened the door between worlds, just as I did long ago. My name is James, and though time has taken me from your side, my love remains. But this letter is not just mine — it is a key for you and for those who come after. Love is never truly lost; it simply waits for the right moment to bloom again."*

Rachel's breath caught, her eyes filling with tears. The letter went on, speaking of patience and hope, of stories yet to be told, and of the promise that love would always find a way across time and space.

As she read, a soft breeze stirred the pages of the nearby journals, as if the room itself was breathing. The scent of roses — faint but unmistakable — filled the air. Rachel folded the letter gently and tucked it inside the locket she wore close to her heart.

The young woman watched her with a curious smile. "Is this place magic?" she asked softly.

Rachel smiled back, her eyes shining. "Maybe it is. Or maybe it's just full of stories waiting to connect us all."

The visitor nodded, settling into a nearby chair, reaching for a pen and a fresh sheet of paper. Rachel felt a quiet joy bloom inside her—the feeling that, even as one story ended, another was just beginning.

And somewhere beyond the walls of *Past Pages*, beneath the watchful stars, the threads of countless lives wove together—endings and beginnings spinning into the eternal dance of love and hope.

Rachel whispered a soft prayer of gratitude, knowing that the letters, the love, and the courage she had found would carry on forever, touching hearts she would never meet.